Barjack

I was riding alongside ~~...~~ a' rocks what set beside a' the road out there, when I seen a gang a' five men riding toward me. I turned and went behint them rocks. I dismounted and tuck my Henry with me. Laying that rifle acrosst a rock, I cranked a shell into the chamber. The riders came to a halt out there in the road.

"Barjack," one of them called out.

"It's me," I answered.

"You might just as well get back on that horse and ride back into town," he said. "No one's getting out."

"You bastards think you can stop me," I said, "you just come right on ahead and try."

He laughed. "You're already stopped," he said. "You ain't going no farther."

I tuck my Henry in my left hand and reached inside my coat with my right to find a stick a' dynamite which I brung out. I helt the fuse to my ceegar tip till it begun to fizzle, and then I helt it a little bit longer. Final, I stood up behint that rock and heaved that son of a bitch just as hard as I could. It went a-flying up and out and landed in the road just in front a' the five a' them . . .

Other *Leisure* books by Robert J. Conley:

BARJACK AND THE UNWELCOME GHOST
NO NEED FOR A GUNFIGHTER
THE GUNFIGHTER
BROKE LOOSE
BARJACK
BRASS
THE ACTOR
INCIDENT AT BUFFALO CROSSING
BACK TO MALACHI

Robert J. Conley

RIO LOCO

Dorchester
Publishing

DORCHESTER PUBLISHING

September 2011

Published by

Dorchester Publishing Co., Inc.
200 Madison Avenue
New York, NY 10016

ISBN 13: 978-1-4285-1174-3
E-ISBN: 978-1-4285-0977-1

The "DP" logo is the property of Dorchester Publishing Co., Inc.

Printed in the United States of America.

Visit us online at www.dorchesterpub.com.

RIO LOCO

Chapter One

I was just setting in my favorite chair in my own saloon, which was knowed as Harvey's Hooch House on account of a previous owner, and I was drinking my favorite whiskey from a big tumbler, and mostly minding my own business, whenever Owl Shit come a-walking in and looking to me like as if he was a-looking for trouble. Course, there wasn't nothing unusual about that. Owl Shit always looked thattaway. He was wearing his six-gun the way he always done. The holster on his loose-fitting belt was hanging right around in the dead center a' the belt right smack in front, so it looked kinda like it was his damn pecker a-hanging down betwixt his legs. I reckoned he had done had him some whiskey somewhere on account a' he seemed to be just a mite drunk already.

He kinda staggered up to the bar and knocked a couple a' men sideways outta his way and banged his fist down on the bar. "Whiskey," he hollered out. Aubrey was plumb down to the other end a' the bar serving a drink to another feller. "Hey," called Owl Shit. "Oberry. You hear me?"

"I'll be right with you, Owl Shit," said Aubrey.

"Now. I want whiskey now."

"I'm coming."

Well, I kinda scooted my chair back so I'd be ready to get up if it turned out to be called for, and I checked my Merwin Hulbert self-extracting revolver to be damn certain it was where I could get at it if I was to have need of it. I picked up my tumbler and had another long swig a' that wonderful stuff. Damn, it was good. I begun to get pissed off that Owl Shit was disturbing my relaxing pleasure.

"Excuse me, sir," said the cowhand on Owl Shit's left, "but that's my drink in front of you."

Whenever Owl Shit had knocked him outta the way, he had stepped up to the bar right there where the feller had been a-standing. Owl Shit looked at the man and picked up the drink. "This'n?" he said.

"Yes."

Owl Shit drank it down and put the glass on the bar in front a' the man. "Thanks," he said. Aubrey come up just then and set a glass in front of Owl Shit and brought out a bottle. He was about to pour a drink when Owl Shit grabbed the bottle outta his hand. "'Bout time," he said.

"Owl Shit," said Aubrey, "we don't want no trouble in here today."

"I ain't going to start no goddamned trouble," said Owl Shit. "Just leave the bottle here with me. That's all."

"You owe me a drink, mister," said the cowhand to Owl Shit's left.

"How'd you come up with that, dumb ass?" said Owl Shit.

"That first drink you had was mine."

"I thanked you for it, di'n't I?"

"Now, see here—"

But the cowhand never got nothing else out. Owl Shit whipped out his Colt and shot him point-blank in the chest. I think he hit him in the heart. Blood spurted out all over Owl Shit and all over the bar, and the poor cowboy leaned back on the bar with both his elbows and a real dumb look on his face. He was done dead. He slid down real slow till he was setting on the floor and leaning back against the bar.

I got up real damn fast and took about four long strides over to the bar. I come up behint Owl Shit as I was hauling out my Merwin Hulbert, and I whacked that damn bastard hard on top a' his head. He stood there rocking for a minute, his head a-bobbing from side to side. Then he started in to turn his head and look at me, but just as he got his head around, he pitched forward, landing hard on the floor. I kicked his Colt across the floor on over to my table. My Bonnie come a-flopping down the stairs about then. "I heared a shot," she said.

"It's took care of," I said. Then I turned to Aubrey. "Aubrey, go find my two worthless depitties and send them down here right away. Bonnie, sweet tits, you get behint the bar till Aubrey gets back."

"Yes, sir, Barjack," said Aubrey.

"And while you're out, send the damn under-taker down."

Aubrey pulled off his apron and headed for the door while Bonnie hustled her fat ass behind the bar. I walked back over to my chair and set back down, picking up my drink and having a long snort. I looked over at the corpus, still bleeding pretty bad, and at Owl Shit laying there flat out on the floor. I drained my glass and held it up high for Bonnie to see. She grabbed my bottle and hurried on over to the table, tits a-bouncing, to refill my tumbler.

I was thinking what a bunch a' shit it was for us in our little town of Asininity to have to put up with the likes a' Owl Shit. He was the younger and worthless brother of ole Chugwater Johnson. Chugwater was all right. He was one of our most prominent citizens. Well, he didn't live right there in Asininity. He had the biggest ranch around, and he lived out there. Owl Shit was always get-ting in some kinda trouble, and Chugwater would bail him out, most usually by pulling out a wad a' bills and paying someone off. There weren't go-ing to be no one to pay off this time. The dead cowhand was a stranger in town, and there was a-plenty a' witnesses in the Hooch House who seen what Owl Shit had did. It was almost for damn sure he would hang this time.

Happy Bonapart and Butcher Doyle, my two depitties, come in just then. I waved them over and pointed to the seeming corpse a' Owl Shit on the floor. "Lug him over to the jail and lock his ass up," I said.

"What's the charge, Barjack?" Happy ast me.

"See that dead corpus over there by him?" I said. "Owl Shit kilt him. What do you think the goddamn charge is?"

"Murder?" said Happy.

"You got it on the first guess," I said. "Now get him over there before he wakes up."

They went to hustling as ole Bones, the undertaker, come in, and I pointed him to his job. "Who's paying for this?" he ast me.

"Marshal's office," I said. Actual it would be the mayor, that damned Peester, but I didn't see no need to go into details with that grave-digging man. Bonnie was busy at the bar with folks who was wanting fresh drinks. My own was about half gone. I would need a refill in a short while. Dingle, the writing feller, come a-walking in, and he come over to my table and set across from me. I waved at Bonnie and she brung him a drink. He tuck a look at ole Bones a-messing with the dead corpse. "What's happened?" he said, hauling out his notebook and his pencil.

"Not much," I said. "Owl Shit come in here and kilt that man without no provocation. That's all."

"Well, where is he?"

"Happy and Butcher hauled his ass to jail," I said.

"They were in here when it happened?"

"No. I had to send for them." I looked up to see that Aubrey had come back. He was tying his apron back on, and Bonnie was headed for my table. She come right to the chair right next to mine and set her wide ass down in it and reached over to grab me and hug me to her in a tight-ass bear hug, most nearly squashing me to death. "That's enough, sweet ass," I said. "Let me a-loose."

"Barjack knocked Owl Shit out cold first," she said to Dingle.

"How you know that?" I said. "You wasn't down here yet."

"Feller at the bar told me," she said. She looked back at Dingle. "Barjack always takes care of trouble whenever it dares to come around where he's at."

Dingle went to scribbling. He had done wrote three or four books about me, and we was both a-making money off of them. Happy and Butcher come back in then, and they both come over to my table. "Set your sorry asses down," I said. I waved at Aubrey. "Have a drink. This here is likely to be the last drink we'll all of us have together here at the Hooch House for a spell."

"How come you to say that, Barjack?" said Bonnie.

"Soon as ole Chugwater hears about his baby brother setting in my jail," I told them, "he'll be a-trying everything he can think about to get him out. We'll have to keep at least one of us down there all the damn time. Maybe two of us."

"He'll hear pretty soon," said Happy. "News travels fast around here."

"We got a couple hours at least," I said.

Aubrey fetched the drinks over to the two dep-itties and I helt my tumbler out to him. He tuck it back to the bar and come back in a hurry with it full again. Dingle was still a-scribbling. We had got to where most a' the time we just ignored him, and he liked it like that.

"Barjack," said Happy, "are we going to have to take Owl Shit over to the county seat to be tried?"

"Nope," I said. "We got us a new percedure here now. We got a judge a-coming to us every two weeks. We'll have the trial right here. And the hanging."

"A real hanging?" said Butcher, who was from New York City.

"Real enough to kill him," I said.

Bonnie give a real big shudder. "What's wrong, pretty ass?" I said.

"The thought of a hanging always gives me the creeps," she said. "What an awful way to die."

"Owl Shit's kinda skinny," I said. "It won't be so bad for him. Just snap his neck if we get a good hangman. Now, for someone built like you, it would be bad. You got too much weight on your butt. It might even jerk your lovely head right off."

She shuddered again. I tuck a long drink. The place was starting in to get lively. Mostly cowhands and local businessmen. I liked that. It meant I was making money. Well, me and Bonnie was making money.

"Marshal?" said Happy, real cautiouslike.

"Yeah?"

"How come Owl Shit to shoot that man in the first place?"

"Meanness," I said.

"Just meanness?"

"That's right."

"Well, what'll you do whenever Chugwater comes in for him?"

"Nothing. Ain't a damn thing I can do. Whenever a man's done locked up and charged with a murder, ain't nothing to be done 'cept to wait for the trial."

"Chugwater ain't a-going to like it," Happy said.

"No," I said. "He ain't. So why don't you finish up your drink and get your ass on down to the jail to keep an eye on things?"

Happy downed his drink and stood up. I likely shouldn'ta made him drink it all down fast like that. He seemed to me to be on kinda wobbly legs. But he got on over to the front door all right and disappeared outta the Hooch House.

"What about me?" said Butcher.

"You're okay for now," I said.

Butcher called for another drink. Bonnie said she had forgot something upstairs and excused herself. She waddled over to the stairs and flung her right foot up on the first stair, and I noticed the way that caused her whole ass end to shift around. Then she swung the other leg and made it shift again. It was kinda like watching a big ship on the ocean getting tossed around by high waves. And I know. I had saw them. I was borned on one a' them oceangoing vessels when my folks was coming over from the Old Country. I hadn't lived out West all a' my damn life. I started out in

New York City, just like ole Butcher Doyle, but I
had left it long before he did.

Well, I never let on to no one, but I was beginning to get some worried about ole Owl Shit's
brother a-coming in to town. I knowed that Chugwater weren't about to let his brother get hanged
up without putting up a fight a' some kind. Now
and then my marshaling job did weigh on me
some. And this was one a' them times. I'll tell you
that for sure. Chugwater had him a bunch a' cowhands out at the ranch who would do any damn
thing he told them to do. They was a loyal bunch
for damn sure. I had done saw him win one big,
rough range war, and them hands a' his fought like
hell for him. I weren't for sure just what he might
do or how far he might go. I was sure about one
thing, though. Whatever he done, it weren't going
to be pretty. And it damn sure weren't going to be
easy for me.

I tuck me another drink, and I seen Bonnie
a-coming back down the stairs. Coming down
she looked a whole lot different from what she
looked a-going up. What caught your eyeballs
when she was coming down was the way her big
tits just bounced up and down. It sure did take
my mind off a' ole Chugwater watching them flop
around like that. She come back over to the table
and flopped her wide ass back down in the chair
next to me and squashed me again with another
bear hug. I struggled loose and had me another
drink a' whiskey. My glass was getting low again.

I didn't even have to wave it. Aubrey tuck notice

all by his lonesome, and I seen him get my bottle and head over to the table. He poured my tumbler full a' whiskey, and then he leaned over to talk into my left ear.

"Barjack," he whispered, "them two cowboys that just left, they work for Chugwater. I betcha they'll ride back to the ranch and tell him what's happened in here. He'll know pretty damn soon."

"Okay," I said. He went back to the bar, and I dranked my drink down as fast as I could. Then I looked across the table at Butcher, and I seen that his drink was about gone too.

"Butcher," I said, "drink up. Let's you and me get our ass down to my office."

My office and the jail was the same. The office had two jail cells in it. When we got there, Happy jumped up from the chair behind my desk he was a-setting at and hurried over to another chair. Butcher found hisself a chair, and I walked over to the gun rack and went to pulling out shotguns. I tossed one to Happy and another to Butcher. Then I helt on to one for my own self. "Check these," I said, "and load them. Hang on to them. You might need them before too much longer. I have a feeling that ole Chugwater will come a-riding in here soon."

Well, we done that, and then I told Butcher to move his chair over against the back wall a' the office and set where he had a clear shot at ole Owl Shit in the jail cell. "If I give you the word," I said, "or if anyone shoots me, kill the bastard."

"Yes, sir," said Butcher.

"What about me, Barjack?" Happy said.

"You just stay where you're at," I said, "and keep your eyes open."

"Yes, sir."

I went back behind my desk and laid my shotgun across it. Then I sat down. I pulled out a desk drawer and got me a tumbler and a bottle and poured me a drink. I don't particularly like to be without one at no time. I tuck a good long drink of it and set it down on the desk.

"When do you reckon he'll get here, Barjack?" said Happy.

"Most any minute now," I said, and just then I heard the sound of several horses riding down the street. I got up, picked up my shotgun, and walked to the window to look out. Sure enough. It were Chugwater and he had five more men with him. They rode right up to the front of the jailhouse and stopped. I stepped out on the boardwalk a-holding that shotgun.

"Howdy, Chugwater," I said.

"Barjack. I hear you got my brother locked up in there."

"That's right."

"I've come to get him out."

"You can't do that."

"How come?"

"He done a killing. Unprovoked."

"Well, can I see him?"

"Sure."

Chugwater swung down out of the saddle, and his boys started to do the same.

"I said you," I told him, kinda lifting the barrel a' my shotgun. "I never said nothing about them."

The cowhands settled back down in their saddles and looked at Chugwater.

"Boys," he said, "go on over to the Hooch House and wait for me there. Have a drink while you're waiting."

They turned their horses and headed for the Hooch House. Chugwater give me a hard look.

"If there was another saloon in town," he said, "I'd have sent them there."

"That's why we ain't got another one," I said. Then I helt the door for him to walk into my marshaling office ahead of me, and he did.

Chapter Two

Whenever we stepped inside the office, ole Chug-water, he stopped just inside the door and turned to look me in the face. I figgered that maybe he was a-trying that ole kid's game, you know, trying to stare me down, so I just stared right back. "Bar-jack," he said, "you know you'll never get away with this."

"I ain't trying to get away with nothing," I said. "The law has caught up with your worthless brother. That's all."

"You mean you have," he said. "You think you're the law around here."

Well, I did kinda think like that, but I weren't going to let him get away with saying it.

"Owl Shit done a killing, a unprovoked kill-ing," I said, "and they was all kinds a' witnesses around when he done it. Now, did you come in here to argue with me, or did you come in to talk to your shit-ass brother?"

"I'd like to talk to him," he said.

I made a gesture toward the jail cell where Owl Shit was standing up and clutching the bars. "Go right ahead," I said. He walked on over there and stood in front of Owl Shit.

"What the hell did you do?" he said.

"I didn't do nothing to get throwed in here," Owl Shit said. "I just shot a feller that we didn't even know on account a' he was smarting off at me. That's all. This crazy stuck-up marshal, he just decided to make it his own business. Now get me out of here."

Chugwater turned his head and looked back at me over his shoulder. Then he looked back at Owl Shit. "I'll get you out. Don't worry," he said. "Just be patient. I can't buy your way out after you done a murder."

"Aw. Come on," Owl Shit said. "You got plenty a' money."

"Money won't do us no good now," Chugwater said. "You're charged with murder."

"So what? It ain't the first time, is it? Get me out."

"Listen, Owl Shit," said Chugwater, lowering his voice, but only it didn't make no difference, we all could hear his ever' word anyhow, "you got to learn to behave yourself. Times is changing. The law's here now. You can't just ride into town no more and have ever'thing your own way. And you're causing me problems trying to take care of you."

"You promised Mama on her deathbed you would do just that. I was there, and I heared you."

"I'll see you later," Chugwater said, and he spun around on his heel and headed for the door. He jerked the door open and turned to look at me once more. "You ain't heard the last of this, Barjack," he said.

"I never thought I had," I told him. He walked on out and slammed the door. Happy come a-walking toward me.

"Barjack," he said, "he means business."

"I reckon I do too," I said.

"You know how many ranch hands he's got?"

"Somewhere between twenty and thirty, I reckon."

Butcher come up outta his chair. "Twenty or thirty?" he said.

"That'd be my guess," I said.

"Well, what are we gonna do?"

"We're going to sit tight right here in my office and jailhouse till the judge gets to town."

"When will that be?"

"I figure he'll be around in about a week now."

"What if Chugwater comes in here with a whole bunch a' cowboys?"

"We'll just have to stand him off."

"We could let him have Owl Shit," said Happy, "and make like he tuck him from us."

"And have the both of them coming into town and drinking right in my own damn saloon, lording it over us? No, thanks. I ain't a-doing that. If either one a' you fine upstanding depitties wants out, now is the time to get to getting. I damn sure don't need you if you don't want to be here."

"I never said that, Barjack," Happy said. "You know I've stuck with you through hard times before. I'll stick this time too."

"Me too," said Butcher, his head hanging low

like he didn't really mean it. "Even if it gets me killed."

"All right, then," I said. "You two stay here and guard the place. If any of Chugwater's boys tries to get in, shoot Owl Shit. I'm going out to try to round us up some help."

"Yes, sir," they both said almost at the same time. I headed outta the place. When I got outside, I could see Chugwater's horse and the horses a' them men what rode in with him all still tied up in front a' the Hooch House. I walked right past them and over to my ex-wife's fancy eating palace. I was hoping to find her new hubby in there. I walked in and she seen me. She give me a real cold look, what woulda froze the face of a polar bear.

"I'm a-looking for the wid—I'm looking for your husband," I said, taking the hat off a' my head, on account a' she was real kinda prissy.

"Mr. Sly is not here," she said. "I believe you will find him at our house."

"Thank you, ma'am," I said, and I put my hat back on and left. I was thinking how what she called "our house" had used to be my house, but I didn't let that stop me. I walked on over to the house, and I found Sly a-setting on the porch a-sunning hisself. I waved a howdy to him.

"Barjack," he said, "what brings you around?"

"I need another depitty or two or three, Sly," I said. "I come to ask you."

"What's the problem?"

"Well, ole Chugwater's baby brother, that low-down sneaky bastard Owl Shit, come into the

Hooch House earlier and shot a man down in cold blood, right in front a' me and a whole mess a' other witnesses. I throwed him in jail. Soon as Chugwater got the word, he come in with some a' his boys and demanded me to turn Owl Shit a-loose. Course, I refused. He said I ain't seen the end a' it. I know he'll be back with a gang and try to shoot Owl Shit outta the jailhouse. I got both Happy and Butcher setting over there right now keeping a eye on things."

Sly stood up, and I seen that he weren't wearing his guns. "Let me go inside and get myself heeled," he said. He went in, and in a couple a' minutes he come back out a-wearing two Colt six-guns. Damn, he looked mean. He was far and wide knowed and feared and called the widda-maker on account a' his skill with them two guns. "Shall I just go on down to the jail?" he asked me.

"Sure," I said, "you can put a chair out on the boardwalk if you like."

I walked back toward town with him for a spell, and when we got close to the Hooch House, he went on toward the jail and I turned aside. I walked to the bar. Aubrey seemed surprised. Chugwater and his bunch was a-setting at a table together, and they all looked hard at me as I walked by. I motioned Aubrey to lean over close, and I said, "Aubrey, is that Churkee and his woman still up in a room here or has they left town yet?"

"As far as I know, Barjack," Aubrey said, "they're still here."

"Which room is they in?"

"Number seven."

I headed for the stairs and run up as fast as ever I could. I walked down the hall to room number 7 and pounded on the door. My legs was a-hurting me from the fast trip up the stairs. Mose Miller, the Churkee, opened the door right away. "Barjack?" he said. "What brings you around?"

I told him what Owl Shit had did in the bar earlier and how I had Happy and Butcher and Sly all over to the jailhouse. I also told him that Chugwater and some a' his boys was just downstairs and what I figgered their intentions was.

"What do you want me to do, Barjack?" he said.

"Buckle on your shooter and get over to the jail," I said. "We need all the help we can get."

His pretty little gal jumped up from off a' the bed and reached for her own shooting iron. "I'll go too," she said. I never argued on account a' I had saw her shoot before, and she could beat most men. That made six of us, and I thought the odds had improved considerable. We was all of us pretty damn good hands with weapons, and three of us, Miller, his woman, and Sly, was goddamn good. Hell, I figgered we could stand off a whole shitting army.

I tuck note a' the fact that Miller had buckled on his own Merwin Hulbert self-extracting revolver, what was just the same as what I carried. He had it because I had recommended it to him, and he had went and bought the last one in the gun shop in Asininity. That there kinda puffed me up a little bit. Well, them two headed for my marshaling office, and I went back downstairs kinda slow and relaxed. I figgered the five a' them could handle any situation what might develop right away.

Chugwater and his little gang was still a-setting down there. As I made my way to my table, Chugwater stood up and walked over. "You're not watching the jail, Marshal," he said.

"What do I need to watch it for?" I said back at him.

He looked back at his little gang and nodded, and they all got up and went outside. "Oh, you just never know what might happen," he said, and he turned and walked to the front door and on outside.

Well, that was all the hint I needed to figger out that he was up to something. Aubrey come bringing me a tumbler full a' whiskey, but I waved him off. "Hold it for me," I said, and I got up and headed for the door. Before I had reached it, I heard some gunshots. When I got out on the boardwalk, I seen two empty horses down in front a' the jail and two bodies on the ground out in the street. I didn't see Sly nowhere. I did see Chugwater at a safe distance away a-watching. The three cowhands what weren't yet kilt were still a-setting on their horses and shooting into the jailhouse.

Then I seen a hand with a six-gun in it poke itself out a winder and fire, and another one of Chugwater's men dropped outta his saddle and plopped in the dirt. They was only just two left, and they turned their horses and commenced to riding away. I stepped out in the street and hauled out my own Merwin Hulbert and tuck careful aim and squeezed the trigger. It were a pretty long shot, but by God, one a' the fleeing bastards throwed his arms up high and tumbled back'ards off his horse. He done a kinda flip and landed on his face, and he didn't move no more. Chugwater caught up with the last one, and the two a' them rode off towards his ranch together.

I walked on down to the jailhouse and went inside. "Anyone hurt?" I said.

"None of us are hit," said Butcher.

"Good," I said. "We kilt four a' them."

"I saw you get that one from down the street," said Sly. "That was a good shot."

"Well," I said, "I couldn't let you all have all the fun, could I?"

"Where was Chugwater?" said Happy.

"He had rode on ahead and was watching from a safe distance," I told them. "Long as he's got cowboys to get shot, he ain't going to put his own self in no danger. Not even for his baby brother."

I said that last loud enough for Owl Shit to hear it too. "Chugwater ain't a-skeered a' you," Owl Shit yelled. "He'll come in here and get you yet."

"Happy," I said, "fetch me a bucket a water outta the back room."

Happy went through the door to the back room. He come back in a minute or so later with a bucket a' water and I looked at it, but I never made to take it off a' him. Instead, I said, "Now throw it on Owl Shit." Happy walked to the cell and slung the bucket, sloshing water all over Owl Shit.

"Goddamn it," Owl Shit said. "You can't treat a prisoner like that. That ain't right. I might catch a goddamn cold in here all wet like this."

"That was just to get your attention," I said. "Now, I don't want to hear no more noise out a' you. The next time you piss me off, it'll be worse. You ain't been fed yet, have you?"

He shuck his head no.

"Well, if you piss me off again, you won't be fed. I'll let you starve in there."

I walked over to my desk and took out the bottle and some glasses, and I poured drinks all around. Sly even took a short one. He never liked to drink in case he was to need use a' his guns. That never bothered me none, though, nor did it bother Happy or Butcher. Even Miller, the Churkee, weren't above having a snort or two just about any time. I think he liked it even more than the rest of us on account a' you wasn't supposed to let a Indian have a drink.

"Well," said Butcher, "I guess we whipped them, all right."

"They'll be back," said Happy.

"How soon, do you think?" Butcher asked.

"I don't believe it will be today," I said. "Sly, why don't you and Churkee and Pistol"—I called Churkee's gal Pistol—"hang around here? Me and these other two will be back after a while."

"All right," Sly said.

I motioned to Happy and Butcher to follow me, and we all went outside. I commenced to leading the way over to the Hooch House.

"Where we going?" said Butcher.

"We're going to the Hooch House to get us a drink," I said.

Chapter Three

The Hooch House was plenty busy. I even had to chase someone away from my own private table, and my Bonnie was a-helping ole Aubrey out behint the bar pouring drinks. She seen me come in, and she come a-bouncing over to the table. "Barjack," she said, setting down beside a' me and hugging me most near to death, "I didn't chase them people away from your own private table on account a' me and Aubrey was so busy back yonder, but I was fixing to just as soon as I got me a chance."

"That's all right, sweet ass," I said. "I tuck keer of it just fine. You want to get us some drinks here?"

She never got up. She just only raised up her arm and waved it around, and ole Aubrey forgot everything what he was a-doing and hurried over with four drinks. He set them around on the table and hurried back to the bar to whatever it was he was a-doing before I so rudely interrupted his ass. I picked mine up and tuck me a good long drink a' that wonderful stuff.

"How come you three to be over here anyhow?"

Bonnie said. "I thought you was a-going to stay in the office as long as you was a-holding Owl Shit in there."

"Churkee and his woman and Sly is all over there," I said. "I think they can handle it all right. We're just taking us a break, is all, from all that there hard work we been a-doing."

"Oh," she said. "I see."

But I got the feeling that she never bought into that there hard work stuff I was a-laying on her. I didn't give a shit, though. I had me another long drink. I slipped my right hand through the stobs in the back a' her chair and grabbed me a hunk a' ass and kinda squeezed on it, and she kinda twitched all over and give me a look. "Barjack," she said, kinda scolding like.

"What, sugar lumps?" I said.

She never answered me then. She just only picked up her little ole pink drink, whatever it was, and tuck a polite sip of it. She ain't never been the same since ole Sly hit town and commenced on his polite ways all the damn time. My curiosity got the better a' me, though. I wondered what that pink shit tasted like, so I picked up her glass and tuck me a swallow. I set the glass back in front a' her and shuddered all over me and made a face.

"Goddamn," I said. "That tastes like parlor woman piss."

Happy and Butcher went to laughing loud. I give them a hard look. Happy, when he could, said, "Barjack, whenever did you taste any parlor woman's piss?"

"I never did," I said, "but if I was to, that there is what it would taste like."

Bonnie whomped me real hard in the ribs with her left elbow and like to knocked me over sideways.

"Damn," I said. "What the hell was that for?"

"For picking on my drink," she said. "I don't never say nothing about what you drink. It ain't nice to pick on what someone likes. How'd you like it if I was to do you that way?"

"Hell, I wouldn't give a damn."

"All right, then," she said, "go on and drink your horse's piss."

I picked up my glass and said, "Be glad to," and I tuck me another gulp. My glass was kinda low by then, and Bonnie, she waved at Aubrey. He seen her and he seen my glass, so she didn't need to holler the way she done. She done that outta meanness. She hollered, "Aubrey, have you collected any more piss outta that damn mule out back?"

Aubrey looked at her kinda weird, like he didn't know what the hell she was talking about.

"Barjack needs some more of it in his glass," she said.

Course, ever'one in the place heard her, and most of them looked at me and went to laughing. I felt my face burn and knowed it turned red. Aubrey brung the bottle over and refilled my tumbler. Bonnie lifted up her glass, and I thought about something to say but decided it would be best to not say it. Instead I said, "Enjoying your pretty pink drink, Bonnie?"

She lifted her glass and tuck a sip. "Yes, indeed I am. Thank you, Marshal. How is your whiskey, dear one?"

"It's just fine," I said. "The damn best whiskey money can buy."

Right about then, I heared some gunshots outside. I couldn't tell exactly from where they was coming, but I had me a idee. They was coming most probable, I figgered, from the jailhouse and my marshaling office. With the trouble I was expecting, I figgered it had to be ole Chugwater or his boys trying to turn Owl Shit a-loose. I tuck me another gulp a' whiskey and set the tumbler down hard on the table.

"Goddamn it," I said. "Happy, you and Butcher go take a look and see where that's a-coming from."

They both jumped up and headed for the door. I had me another slurp a' that wonderful stuff and waited. In another minute, Butcher come back to the table. He didn't set down, though. "Barjack," he said. "There's four men out front in the street on horseback. They're holding their guns on Happy. They want you to come out."

"Where'd them shots come from?" I said.

"Oh," he said. "Down at the jail."

Well, I shoved back my chair and stood up.

"Barjack," Bonnie said, "be careful."

"You know me," I said, "I'm always careful. Go on back out there with Happy," I said to Butcher.

"Yes, sir," he said, and he headed back for the door. I went to walking toward the back door. I cussed myself as I went on account a' it was just

only ole Happy what had the sense to tote along
the shotgun I had give him. Mine and Butcher's
was both back in my office. I went out the back
door and walked around the building. On the
way, I hauled out my trusty Merwin Hulbert
forty-five-caliber self-extracting revolver and helt
it ready. When I come to the front corner a' the
building, I slowed my ass down. I peeked out
around the corner and tuck me a look. Them four
men was setting on their horses with their guns
out a-looking down at Happy and Butcher and
not looking in my direction a'tall.

I tuck a bead on one man's back and stepped
out in the street. I pulled the trigger just as I hollered, "Put them guns down or I'll shoot." I hit
the son of a bitch right smack in the middle a' his
back. He twitched and dropped his weapon and
fell off a' his horse, plopping hard on the street.
His horse went to jumping around. The other
three all looked in my direction, and when they
done that, Butcher and Happy both went to shooting. I shot one more time too, and I dropped another one. I seen both a' the other two fall, but I
don't know who shot which one.

"Make sure they're dead," I said, and my two
depitties went out in the street to kick the bodies
and make certain. I walked on around to join
them.

"They're dead all right, Barjack," Happy said.

"Good, let's check the jailhouse." There was
still shots coming from that direction, and we commenced walking thattaway. The men down at the
jail wasn't setting on their horses. They was dis-

mounted and hiding around somewheres. On our way down there, I tried to locate them. I seen one behint a watering trough in the street. I knowed that ole Happy was a good shot with a handgun from a fairly long distance. "Happy," I said.

"Yes, sir?"

"See that feller crouched down behint the watering trough down yonder?"

"I see him."

"Can you pick him off from here?"

"I reckon I can."

"Well, do it, then, goddamn it," I said.

Happy stopped walking and handed his shotgun to me. I tuck it. He leaned up against a post what was holding the overhanging roof up over the boardwalk and he pulled out his Colt. He cocked it and stretched out his arm, and he put his left hand underneath it to steady it. He tuck a while aiming, and I was about to tell him to hurry it on up, but then he pulled the trigger. The rat down there behint the trough jerked. Then he stood up and leaned over forward, and then he fell, his top half hanging down in the water. Water sloshed out over the edges a' the trough.

"Good shot, Happy," I said.

"Damn good," said Butcher.

"Do either one a' you see any a' the other ones?" I asked them.

They didn't answer me right off. They was a-looking around.

"Marshal," said Happy, "I think one might be hiding in there in the doorway to the hardware store."

I handed him back his shotgun. "Spray the doorway with this here scattergun," I said. "Wait till we get a little closer, though."

We walked on, and whenever Happy figgered we was close enough, he raised the shotgun to his shoulder and pointed it in the general direction a' the hardware store. He pulled the trigger, and that shotgun roared. Pellets musta been dancing all around the store. A cowhand come a-yelping out into the open, hopping and a-dancing. Me and Butcher both commenced shooting with our six-guns, and he was hit several times. Final, he dropped down dead on the boardwalk. Two more come a-running out from somewheres then and headed for their horses.

I seen a arm poke outta one of the windows in my office and fire a shot, and one a' the bastards dropped off a' his horse. Then Sly come out onto the boardwalk and leveled his deadly Colt at the last one what was riding hard outta town, and he shot him right outta the saddle. We walked on down and checked all a' the bodies. They was all dead. We never had no time to not kill them. "Butcher," I said, "go find Bones and tell him to clean up the street."

Butcher tuck off in a run. Sly walked over to me. "You showed up in the nick of time, Barjack," he said.

"Hell, four of them come down to the Hooch House to get me," I told him.

"That makes eight," Sly said. "Chugwater's serious about this."

"It's his baby brother we got in a cell in there," I

said. "And if we keep him there till the judge shows up, he'll damn sure hang."

"I think I could use a drink," Sly said.

Well, that surprised me. I hadn't never heared ole Sly actual call for a drink. "There's a bottle in my desk," I said. "Come on."

We went in, and I got the bottle and some glasses outta my desk drawer. I poured drinks all around, and ever'one tuck a chair till I run out. "That's all right," Miller, the Churkee, said. "We'll sit in here." He tuck his sweetie by her arm and led her into the unused jail cell, where they set down on the cot and went to sipping on their whiskey. Sly slugged his down real fast and held the glass out to me.

"I believe one more is called for," he said.

"You goddamn right," I said, and I poured his glass full a second time. He tuck a sip, and then he said, "Barjack, don't you think it's time we made some plans?"

"I sure do, Widdamaker," I said. "But let's wait for Butcher to get back, so we don't have to go all over it again."

Just about then, Butcher did come back. There weren't no more chairs, so I told him to set on the edge a' my desk, and I poured him a drink. He perched his ass down.

"All right," I said, "ever'one listen up. We got us a serious situation here. Chugwater hit us with eight men, and it didn't work. Next time, he'll use a larger force. We got to be ready for it. Happy, you and Butcher take turns a-setting on the roof. I think you can see from up there if anyone's a-coming into town from the direction a' Chugwater's ranch. I want one a' the two a' you up there all the time."

"Yes, sir," said Happy. Butcher nodded.

"Pistol."

"Right here," she said from inside the cell.

"I want you to set out here with a shotgun and keep it trained on Owl Shit all the time."

"When do I shoot him?" she asked me.

"Any time Chugwater's boys gets inside a' the office. I don't want them setting him free. I want him dead first."

"I'll do it," she said, looking straight at Owl Shit through the bars. I ain't for sure, but I think that Owl Shit was a-trembling then.

"Sly, Miller, and me will just hang around in here most a' the time. We'll let one a' the three of us go out at a time to eat a meal or get a drink or whatever. But just one at a time. That means at least three of us will be in here all the time."

"And one on the roof," said Butcher.

"That's right," I said, "and one on the roof."

"Now, don't no one let no one else in here, 'cept only the rest of us. That's all. And if you're out and come back, holler out and identify yourself before you come a-walking in here. If you don't, you'll get your ass kilt. Pistol."

"What?"

"If that there door starts to open and no one's called out, I want you to shoot. You got that?"

"I sure have."

"Don't even wait to see who it is. Just if that door handle moves, shoot. We'll look and see who it is later."

"I got you."

"We're even going to sleep here," I said. "Three of us at a time. I don't want no one sneaking in on us after dark. And if there's three of us in here at night, one can stay awake."

"Barjack," said Sly, "may I request the first night off? I'd like to go home and explain to Lillian what's going on."

"Yeah. Sure," I said, thinking to my own self, let her wonder. To hell with her. But I never said nothing like that out loud to the old widdamaker. "Happy, you want to take the first watch up on top?"

"Sure," he said.

"Well, get your ass on up there, then," I said, and he picked up his shotgun and hurried on out the door. I turned back to Sly then and said, "Sly, you might as well go on to see your wife."

"Thank you, Barjack," he said, and he tipped his hat and went out the door. Damn, he was po-lite. I shoulda been thanking him for throwing in with us on this deal. With them two gone, that left me and Butcher and the Churkee and his woman, Pistol. I thought about going back to the Hooch House and my Bonnie, but something come over me real hard like a sense a' duty or something else awful like that. I just leaned back in my chair and picked up my glass a' whiskey and tuck a drink. Then it went real quietlike in the marshaling office.

Chapter Four

Pistol Polly was still a-setting with Churkee on the jail cot in the unused cell. She was a-twirling her six-gun on her trigger finger. I was setting behint my desk a-watching her. Then she let that there six-gun go, and it went a-flying up high. Whenever it come back down, she caught it by the handle and helt it ready to shoot. I hadn't never saw a man do nothing that fancy. I waited till she shoved it back into the holster, and then I said, "Pistol."

"Yes, sir."

"Didn't I told you to set out here with a shotgun?"

"Yes, you did," she said, a-getting up and going for the shotgun. She planted her ass right where I had told her to, and set down, shifting her eyeballs from Owl Shit in his cell to the front door and back again. Churkee went to sleep pretty soon, and then so did Butcher. I ast Pistol if she needed to catch some snoozes, but she told me to go on ahead. She was wide awake. I dropped off pretty quick a-setting there at my desk.

I don't know just how long I had been a-sleeping whenever I was rudely awoke by a loud goddamn noise. It sounded like the sky a-falling. I like to fell over in my chair, but I never. Instead I jumped up, grabbing the shotgun off a' the top a' my desk. I jerked it up ready to shoot and looked around, but I never saw nothing. The front door was still closed. Pistol had come up off a' her chair and was a-looking into Owl Shit's cell.

"What was that?" I said.

Churkee come a-running outta the other cell with his six-gun out.

"It come from in there," Pistol said, jerking he shotgun toward Owl Shit's cell.

I tuck the cell keys from off a' my desk and walked over to the door. "Get your ass over there against that wall, Owl Shit," I said, and he moved where I told him to move to. "Pistol, shoot him if he moves."

"With pleasure," she said.

I unlocked the door and went in. Nothing seemed wrong in there a'tall. I kept on a-looking around for a bit. Then I decided to look out the winder, and when I looked thattaway, I seen that there was ropes looped around and around the winder bars. I moved on over to the winder kinda cautiouslike and peered out. It were dark and I couldn't see none too clearly out there, but I seen a big pile a' something on the ground. I went back outta the cell and locked the door back. I tossed the keys onto the top a' my desk and headed for the front door.

"Butcher," I said, "come on with me." He follered me. "Keep a sharp look," I said to Churkee and Pistol. Then I went out the front door with Butcher.

We was each of us a-holding our shooters ready for action as we went creeping around to the side a' the jail. I didn't see no one around there, but what I did see was kinda comical-like. Them ropes was stretched out to two saddle horns. One saddle was a-laying on the ground. It musta ripped right off a the horse's back. The horse wasn't nowhere in sight. The other saddle had stayed on the horse, but the horse had been pulled over on its damn side. It was just a-laying there on the ground and trying to stand back up. No cow-hands was in sight nowhere.

I stepped out into the street and yelled up at Happy up on the roof. "Happy," I called out.

"Yes, sir."

"Did you see any cowboys ride in here?"

"No, sir," he said. "I never."

"Damn," I said, and then just kinda to my own self but out loud, I said, "The silly bastards'll try any damn thing." I looked at Butcher, who was just a-standing there a-scratching his head. "Go on up there and spell Happy," I said.

"Yes, sir," he said, and he hustled off to climb up on the roof. In a few minutes Happy come on down and stopped beside a' me. I was still in the street just a-looking around. I was wondering where two cowboys without no horses mighta got to.

"Go on in, Happy," I said, "but call out before you touch that door."

"Yes, sir," he said, and he stepped up onto the boardwalk and yelled, "It's Happy coming in. Don't shoot."

"Come on in, Happy."

He opened the door and went inside. I follered him and when I come to the door, I yelled, "Barjack coming in."

"Come ahead, Marshal."

I went in, and I latched the door back.

"Barjack?" said Happy.

"Yeah."

"Chugwater ain't waiting none at all. That was his third try all in one day."

"You're right," I said.

"He might could even try again before morning."

"Three or two times," I said. "We'll just hope Butcher's eyes is better than what you got."

"What do you mean, Barjack?"

"Well, hell, two cowboys just tried to tear the wall outta my jail, and you never even seen them come into town. Did you?"

Happy hanged his head down like he was embarrassed or ashamed, and he said, "No, sir. I never."

Well, Chugwater never tried again that night, and come morning, ole Sly come up to the jailhouse. He yelled out his name and we told him to come on in. "Any action last night?" he asked.

"Two cowboys roped up the bars in Owl Shit's winder and tried to pull them out," said Pistol, "but it never worked. One horse went down and the other saddle got jerked off a' the horse."

"What about the cowboys?"

"We never seen hide nor hair of them," I said.

"Well," Sly said, "I asked Lillian to have six

breakfasts fixed up and sent over. They'll be here before long."

"Thanks, Mr. Sly," said Pistol.

"I'll put some coffee on here," Pistol said. "If I can move, Barjack."

"Go on ahead, Pistol," I said. She put her shotgun down and went to build a pot a coffee.

"Sly," I said, "did you see any a' Chugwater's boys in town when you was a-coming over?"

"No," he said. "I didn't see a one of them."

"Well," I said, "right now I'm making up a new rule. If anyone sees Chugwater or any of his hands in town, arrest them and fetch them over here to the jail. If they refuse to come along peaceful, kill them."

"What charge, Barjack?" said Happy.

"Never mind that," I said. "Just do it."

"Yes, sir."

Well, I set back down behint my desk and went back to sleep in a short while, and by God, I dreamt about them two times I had went flying, not in my dreams, mind you, them two times in real life when I had flew. If you ain't read my other books, you might not believe it, but I had for real learnt how to fly, and I had did it twice. I never learnt how to land real good, though. I can tell you, it were a real hair-raising experience, that flying. When I come to, I thunk I would like to try it again one a' these days. Maybe I could land better if I was to do it again.

Well, Pistol was the one what was awake, and so I told her to go on ahead and get her some sleep. I would keep watch, but then ever'one else

went to waking up. It was morning already. Pistol
went into the free cell and gouged ole Churkee up
off a' the cot, and then she laid down on it to catch
her some winks. She hadn't got to sleep much,
though, till the man from Lillian's snooty eating
place come a-bringing our breakfasts. Sly had
warned them, so when he come up to the door, he
hollered out, "Don't shoot me. It's breakfast."

"Let him in," I said, and Churkee went over
and unlatched the door. He come in all loaded
down, and I let him unpile the stuff onto my desk.
Ever'one went to eating. The disturbance had woke
up ole Pistol, and she got herself some too. Whenever Happy had done finished, I tole him to go
take Butcher's place on the roof and tell Butcher to
come on down and have some chow. He went out,
and pretty soon Butcher come in to eat. Whenever
we was all did, I had Butcher to gether up the dirty
dishes and stuff and take it back over to Lillian's
place. I felt some better and had me another cup a'
coffee. Soon as I finished with it, I poured myself a
glass full a' good whiskey. I tuck a good long
slurp and then I did feel a whole lot better.

Setting there with my whiskey, I got to thinking. I wondered about going out to the Johnson
Ranch and arresting Chugwater. That would sure
enough put a stop to all this bullshit. But then I
recalled what a army a' cowpunchers he had out
there, and I decided that it sure as hell wouldn'ta
been worth the try. I guessed there weren't nothing for it but just what we was already doing. We
had done stood off three tries, so I guessed we

could stand off more. We had us about six more days to go, was all. Hell, yes, we could do it.

It was going to get mighty lonesome, though, living in that there office and jail without my sweet-ass Bonnie Boodle to keep me company. I was already missing her a whole damn bunch. Them great big titties was sure nice to snuggle up inside of. I got cold just a-thinking about all that warmness I was a-missing. I quick took me another long shot a' whiskey, and it warmed me up some. I decided that I had to think a' something else besides my Bonnie's honey lips. I had best be a-thinking about ole Chugwater.

The trouble was that I had done thunk about Chugwater so much that there wasn't nothing else to think about. Just then somebody jerked on the door and woulda jerked it plumb open if it hadn't a' been latched. Pistol fired off her shotgun and blowed a hole clean through the door. I heared a yelp from outside while shotgun pellets was a-bouncing all over the office.

"Goddamn it," come a voice from outside. "Don't murder me. It's Dingle."

"Well, hell," I said, "let Dingle in."

Dingle hadn't been around whenever I told ever'one to yell before coming in. Churkee opened the door and Dingle come in looking white as a sheet and trembling like a scared dog.

"Why'd you try to kill me?" he said.

"I reckon you never got the word, Dingle," I said. "I told Pistol there to shoot first and ask questions later if anyone tried to come in without hollering out his name first. Chugwater has tried to bust his brother out three times already."

"I'm sorry," Pistol said, and she sounded like she really meant it too.

"You just done what I told you to do," I said. "You don't need to go apologizing for it."

"Are you hurt?" she said.

"No," Dingle said. "I don't think so."

His hat and his notepad both had some fresh holes in them, though. I told him to come on in and set, but he tossed his notepad on my desk and said, "I'll be right back."

"Where you going?" I said.

"To the outhouse."

"Holler out before you try to come back in."

"Don't worry about that," he said, hurrying back out the door.

"Barjack, I might have killed him," Pistol said.

"If it happens again," I said, "do the same damn thing."

"But—"

"Just do it. It wouldn'ta been no great big loss nohow."

Churkee walked over to Pistol Polly and tuck the shotgun from her. He put an arm around her shoulder. "Go on back to the cot and get some sleep," he said. "I'll take your place."

She looked at me and said, "Barjack?"

"Go on," I said. "It's all right."

She went on into the cell and laid her ass down on the cot. I think she was asleep right fast. Churkee set down on her chair a-holding that shotgun.

"Barjack?" come a wheedling little voice from Owl Shit.

"What the hell do you want?" I said.

"Can I have a cup a coffee, please?" he said.

"Someone fetch him a cup," I said.

Butcher was back by then, and he went and poured a cup full a' hot coffee and tuck it over to the cell. He handed it through the bars to Owl Shit. Owl Shit said, "Thank you," and it come to me that mighta been the first time in his whole life he had said that. He set down on his cot and went to sipping on it. I thought that if we hadda throwed his ass in jail and been mean to him the way we was a-being a whole hell of a long time ago, he might just be a nice fella by now. Them was the first words he had said since I had throwed that bucket a' water on him and told him to keep his mouth shut.

Butcher was still over by the cell. He said, "Owl Shit?"

Owl Shit looked up over his cup. "Yeah?" he said.

"How come you let ever'one call you by that nasty name, Owl Shit?"

"I don't know," Owl Shit said. "They went to calling me that when I was just a little snot. Called me that ever since."

"You got a real name?" said Butcher.

"I got one."

"Well, what is it?"

"You won't tell no one, will you?"

"No. I sure won't."

Owl Shit just almost whispered then. "It's Merwin," he said. "Merwin Johnson."

"That ain't a bad name," said Butcher. "I bet your mama give it to you."

"I think so," said Owl Shit.

"Ever'one calls me Butcher, but my real give name is Harvey," Butcher said. "Mama give it to me. I don't think daddies ever give names like that to kids. Do you?"

"I don't think so. Harvey."

"Now, you keep that kinda quiet. I ain't going to go telling your name around."

"I won't tell," Owl Shit said.

Butcher suddenly turned to face me. "Barjack," he said. "What's your first name?"

"Marshal," I said.

"No, for real," said Butcher.

"I don't reckon you nor no one else needs to know it."

"Oh, come on. Me and Owl Shit has told ours to each other."

"That's your business. Mine is mine."

"What if you was to get killed?" Butcher said. "Or just drop dead one a' these days. What the hell would we put on your tombstone? Just Barjack?"

"You can put whatever you like on my tombstone," I told him. "I won't give a shit on account a' I won't be around to read it."

Chapter Five

Well, hell, I couldn't take it no more. The next night I made sure there was a-plenty a' depitties hanging around the jailhouse, and then I went back over to the Hooch House to find my sweet Bonnie. I found her sure enough, and I walked over to stand beside her there at the bar and I give her a squeeze. She kinda jumped and shrieked on account a' she hadn't seen me come in, but whenever she turned her head and seen me, she give me one a' her damned big bear hugs. She like to've squoze the life outta me too. Final she cut out the squeezing and turned me a-loose, and I sucked in a bunch a' air to replenish my poor ole lungs.

"Barjack," she said, "is ever'thing all right? How come you to be over here?"

"Ever'thing's under control," I said. "I got a bunch a' depitties over to the jail a-watching things. I just got to missing you is all."

I shouldn't ought to 'a' said that, on account a' it got to her, and she slung her arms around me again and went to squishing on me. It tuck ever'thing I had in me to stand that bear hug twice in a row so close like, but I done it. Just then Aubrey put my

tumbler on the bar in front a' me, and it was
plumb full a' good brown whiskey. I hadn't called
for it, but then, I didn't need to with ole Aubrey. I
picked it up and tuck me a good long swaller to
help me get over them bear hugs. Then I set it
back down.

"Honey tits," I said, "what do you say me and
you go up to our private love nest upstairs for a
spell?"

"I'm ready, sweetness," she said.

I picked up my tumbler and wrapped my extra
arm around her big waist and we started in walking toward the stairs. When we got there, she
moved a little faster'n what I could, and so she got
some ahead a' me. I let her, so that I could slip my
hand down and grab on to one great big cheek a'
her ample ass. It wobbled up and down and from
side to side while I was a-squeezing on it. I tell
you what, if I weren't already ready for action,
that sure as hell got me there. When we got up to
the top a' the landing, she hurried on to open the
door to our room, but I just stood there for a bit
a-catching my breath. Hell, I had walked plumb
from the marshaling office to the Hooch House,
and then in just another minute, I had walked up
the damn stairs. I was near wore out. But then
I follered her over to the room where she had
done gone in and I went in after her.

I tell you something, that big woman could really move fast whenever she tuck a mind to. She
had done wriggled her massive self outta her dress
and tossed it aside. I tuck off my hat and tossed it.
Then I follered it with my jacket and my vest and

my shirt. I set down to pull off my boots, and then Bonnie, stark-staring nekkid, was over in front a' me and down on her knees a-helping me. In a half a minute she had me as nekkid as she already was. Then she grabbed me by my both hands and pulled me up to my feet. Oh, that made my legs hurt some. She helt me up, though, with another bear hug, and a minute later, she dragged me over to the bed and throwed me down on it.

Well, I weren't quite ready, but she got me that-taway real fast, and then she climbed on and like to wore me out. I could tell I weren't the man I used to be, but what the hell? She was happy, so I reckon I done all right. "Where's my drink?" I said. She lumbered her ass outta the bed and waddled over to the table where I had set it whenever I come in. She brung it back to me.

"Here it is, sweetness and light," she said.

I tuck it and drained the glass, and she went right back to the table and opened the drawer and hauled out my bottle what I kept up there. Then she come back over to the bed and poured my glass full again.

"Thank you, sugar twat," I said.

She wallered back into the bed and on top a' me, and she mashed me so much that I couldn't hardly swaller. I did manage, though, to get down a couple a' good gulps. Well, we romped around a little bit more and I finished off my glass a' whiskey. She leaned down over me and kissed me full on the face with her big slobbery lips, and then she said, "Barjack, you wanna take a nice bubbly bath with me?"

"Sounds loverly," I said, so she ordered up one and pretty damn soon we had us a big tub a' hot water right there in the middle a' the room. We pulled a couple a' straight chairs over beside the tub so we'd have us some tables, and I lit me a cigar and put the ashtray on one a' the chairs. Then I poured my glass back full and set it by the ashtray. Bonnie got a bottle a' something and poured a bunch of it into the water, and then she clumb over the edge and settled down. The level a' the water rose up considerable then, and then she went to swishing her arms around, and the bubbles commenced to developing.

I climbed in and settled down betwixt her legs, and the water riz up some more. I was damn near afraid that we'd slosh it over onto the floor, but we never. I puffed on my cigar and had me a drink and let my ass slide down as deep as I could get. "I got to admit, sweetness," I said, "that this here was a damn good idee you had."

"Umm," she moaned. "It does feel good, don't it?"

"Yes, indeedy," I said.

She went to soaping up on me, and she soaped me all over, and I mean, all over. I reckon I hadn't never been so clean in my whole entire damn life as what she made me just then. Then I done her the same favor, and Lordy but it was fun. Whenever we was both washed good, I just laid back in the hot water with my both hands on her great fat thighs and stroked them real slowlike. And then, by God, I went to sleep right there in the goddamn bathtub full a' hot and bubbly water.

I never woked up till Bonnie were lifting me bodily outta the water. "Hey," I said, "what're you a-doing?"

"Just relax, Barjack," she said, and she dropped me over onto the bed, where she had done laid out several towels. Then she went to rubbing me dry. She had already done got herself outta the tub and dried her ass off and put on her frilly, flimsy little robe. I could see right through it too. I pinched her titties while she was a-rubbing on me.

Well, now, she dressed me back up in nice clean clothes, and I strapped on my Merwin Hulbert, and she wriggled her ass back into a dress, and then we walked back down the stairs and went over to my private table. Aubrey brung us our drinks, my whiskey and Bonnie's pretty little pink thing, whatever it was. I thought about a remark I could make, but I decided not to make it. We was both a-feeling so good that I sure as hell didn't want to do nothing to spoil the atmosphere.

"Thank you, Aubrey," she said.

"Yes, ma'am," he said. He went back behint the bar.

"Barjack?" Bonnie said.

"What?"

"Lookit the clock."

I glanced over at it a-hanging on the wall behint the bar, but I never thunk nothing about it. "Yeah," I said.

"It's near morning," she said.

"What?"

"We been making love all night long."

I looked at the clock again, and she was right,

by God. We sure as hell had played the whole night away. "Damned if you ain't right," I said. I tuck another swig. Bonnie picked up her little pink drink with her thumb and two fingers with her little finger a-sticking out to the side and had her a dainty little sip. It made me think about Sly again. Then Dingle come in through the front door. He come right back to my table and set down across from me.

"Barjack," he said.

"That's my damn name."

"Barjack, Happy sent me over here. He said I should go because I'm the only one you didn't deputize."

"You mean he throwed you out?"

"Well, no, but he wanted me to tell you what's going on."

"I'm a-listening," I said.

"Well, it seems that Chugwater and a whole bunch of his cowboys are hanging around town."

"That's it?" I said. "Just hanging around?"

"Well, yes. But they've been here all night."

"So the wolves is gethering, are they?"

"It sure does look that way."

"Barjack?" said Bonnie. "Does this mean trouble?"

"I don't reckon it means much trouble," I said. "They'll find out that there ain't no sheep what they're gethering around."

But to tell you the whole truth a' the matter, I was a-feeling kinda like a sheep with the wolves a-gethering around me. That there news what Dingle had brung sure as hell weren't the best news I coulda heared just at that damn time. I figgered what with the men we had done kilt that ole Chugwater could round up at least twenty men if he wanted that many. I helt back a shudder at the thought. I picked up my tumbler and emptied it right then, and I shoved back my chair to stand up.

"I reckon I'd best get on down to the jailhouse," I said.

"You do think there's trouble a-coming," Bonnie said.

"Nothing for you to worry your pretty little fat face over," I said. "I just think I'd oughter go down and talk with my depitties about the situation. That's all."

"Barjack, be careful," she said.

"That's my middle name, sweet tits," I said. "Come on, Dingle. Let's get our ass back down there."

We walked out onto the boardwalk together and turned to head for the jailhouse. Just as we turned, a bullet smacked into the wall just beside a' my head. I jerked out my Merwin Hulbert and looked around. They was two cowhands a-standing out in the street. Both of them had their Colts out and a-pointed at me and Dingle. I shoved Dingle outta the way back toward the door to the Hooch House.

"Watch out, Barjack," he shouted.

"Barjack," one a' the cowhands said, "your ass is grass, and I'm a hungry bull."

I snapped off a lucky shot and dropped the hungry bull right in the street where he had been a-standing. The other one shot then, but I had dodged to one side. His bullet smacked into the wall alongside the other'n. I raised up my Merwin Hulbert and aimed at him, but he had turned around and was a-running. I aimed real keerful, and then I pulled the trigger. My shot hit him in the right cheek a' his ass. He screamed and went to tumbling in the street. He was on his belly, and he kinda raised hisself up on his right hand. I fired again, and this time I hit him smack in the middle a' his back. He dropped down on his face dead.

"Come on, Dingle," I said, and we hurried on down to the jailhouse. Whenever we got there, I damn near forgot to yell out. My hand was on the door handle whenever I remembered.

"Barjack a-coming in," I called out. Then I pulled on the door, but it were latched. In another minute, someone unlatched it, and I went in, follered by Dingle. Pistol Polly was a-setting in that chair with her shotgun pointed at the door. I heaved a heavy sigh and shut the door behint me. Dingle latched it back.

"We heard shooting," Sly said.

"I just kilt a couple a' cowhands what was taking potshots at me," I said.

"They're all over town, Barjack," said Happy.

"That there's just what I come back to talk with you about," I said. I went back behint my desk and set down. The first thing I done was to open up my desk drawer and get out my bottle and some glasses. I poured some drinks around. Sly turned it down.

"What are we going to do?" said Polly.

"If you get a shot at one, kill him," I said.

"Without he's doing nothing wrong?" said Happy.

"They're all in town to get Owl Shit outta jail," I said. "That there is wrong enough, ain't it?"

"Well, I guess."

"All I done just now was to come walking outta the Hooch House," I said, "and two of them went to shooting at me. I was just lucky, is all. We ain't going to wait for them to shoot first no more. When you see them, kill them."

"Yes, sir," said Happy.

Sly was standing at the winder kinda looking out sideways. "It looks like they're all going into the Hooch House," he said.

"Good," I said. "Maybe I'll get most a' their money before we have to kill them dead."

Churkee stepped over to my desk then, and he said, "So, does that mean that we just sit in here and wait till we get a shot at each one of them?"

"That's about the only thing that I can see that we can do," I said. "Does any one a' you have any other idee? I'd be glad to hear it if you do."

No one said anything, so I just tuck me a drink, was all. Sly was still a-watching out the winder. "Where's Butcher?" I said.

"He's on the roof," Happy said.

"Good. That's just where he'd ought to be. Anyone seen Chugwater?"

"I saw him go into the Hooch House with his boys," Sly said.

Of a sudden, I begun to worry about my Bonnie. Would Chugwater mess with her? I wondered. I didn't think so, but then you never know what a bastard will do whenever he gets desperate. I thunk about taking all my posse over to the Hooch House, but then, who would watch the jail? I didn't have enough men to split them up neither. Not against that bunch of Chugwater's. I drank my whiskey on down fast and poured me another glass full. I thunk to my own self, If that Chugwater bothers my Bonnie, there'll be hell to pay. I won't kill him. Not right off. I'll tie his ass up and strip his skin off. Real slow. I'll skin him alive and tack his hide up right in front of him, him there all raw and bleeding. He had ought to know it too, and if he knows it, he'll leave her alone and just only pay for his damn drinks over there, is all.

"Dingle," I said.

"Yes."

"Has any a' them seen you with us? Besides them two I just kilt, I mean."

"I don't think so."

"Then you'd oughta be safe out there. I want you to go back over to the Hooch House and set in a corner and keep your eyes and ears open. If anything happens that hadn't ought to, come back over here and tell me."

"I'll do it," he said, and he headed for the door.

"Wait a minute," I said. I got up and tuck a Webley Bulldog pocket pistol outta my gun rack and I dropped it into his coat pocket. "Go out the back door," I said.

"Okay." He turned and went out through the back room. He was a-carrying his notepad with him.

Polly said, "Barjack, will he be all right?"

"I think so," I said. "They don't know that he's with us. He's just only a scribbler, is all. They won't mess with him."

"Barjack," said Sly, "what if I was to slip out the back and sneak around to see if I get a chance to take any of them out, one at a time? Narrow the odds, so to speak."

I rubbed my chin and give it a thought. It seemed like not a bad idee. "I think there's enough of us in here," I said. "It sure as hell couldn't hurt nothing. All right. Go on ahead."

He headed into the back room.

Chapter Six

Well, now, let me tell you what. I were uncomfortable. I had ole Butcher up on top a' the jailhouse a-watching, and ole Dingle down at the Hooch House a-watching and a-listening, and now ole Sly out a-hunting lone cowboys to kill, and there I was just a-setting in the office killing time with my rest of the depitties and that damned ole Owl Shit setting in the can. I felt kinda like I had ever'body else out a-doing my work for me. Then I thunk about it a little bit deeperlike. It come to me that maybe that there was just the way it had ought to be. Being town marshal, I had a lot a' responsibilities, and I had the job a' delegating that there responsibility too. You might even say that were the mainest part a' my job. That there delegating. Why, hell, I weren't s'posed to do ever'thing. I felt some better whenever I seen it like that. Yes, sir. It seemed almost like as if I weren't s'posed to do nothing a'tall. I poured myself another glass full a' whiskey and relaxed.

"I wish we could be doing something," Churkee said all of a sudden.

"We're a-doing all we can do for now," I said.

"Barjack?" said Happy.

"What?"

"Do you think we can hold out here against all a' them Chugwater hands till the judge gets here?"

"Hell, yes," I said. "We been doing all right so far, ain't we? Ain't we got ole Sly, the widdamaker, with us? And Churkee and Polly over there. Ain't they top guns? And then you and Butcher ain't no slouches. And how about me? Hell, I've got books writ about me, ain't I?"

"Yes, sir," Happy said.

"Just who the hell is Chugwater anyhow? He's just a old rancher. A cowpuncher. That's all. He ain't nothing to worry about."

"I guess not," Happy said. "He's sure got a bunch a' men working for him, and if they ain't enough, he's got the money to hire more whenever he wants to."

"Hell, I've got money, ain't I? I'm one a' the wealthiest men in Asininity, ain't I? Chugwater ain't got nothing on me. No, sir. He's just got that damn funny name, is all. Chugwater. I don't know if he's named after that damn crick what runs by the edge a' town or if the crick was named after him. I ain't for sure. But that ain't no claim to fame no-how. Chugwater. Named after a crick what's dry for more than half a' the year."

"Chugwater Crick," Happy kinda mused. "Funny. I never even thought about that before."

"Well, you think about it. Don't it seem silly to be a-worrying over a man with a dumb name like that? Chugwater."

"Barjack, that Chugwater Crick runs through

here from plumb out to Chugwater's ranch, don't it?"

"I reckon it do," I said.

"That's funny," he said. "Do you reckon his mama named him Chugwater?"

"How'd I know?"

"Can I say something, Marshal?"

I looked around right quick at Owl Shit there in the cell. It were him what ast that question. "What the hell do you want?" I said.

"I just asked you if I can say something, 'cause I don't want to get no water throwed on me."

"Go on and say it," I told him.

"She never done that."

"Who? What are you talking about?"

"Mama. She never named him Chugwater. What kind of a mama would name a kid Chugwater?"

"She never?" said Happy.

"No. She never."

"So what the hell did she name him?"

"Charlton," said Owl Shit.

I bursted out a-laughing so hard that I like to fell outta my chair. Whenever I kinda caught my breath again, I tuck out another glass and poured it full a' whiskey. "Happy," I said, holding it out, "give this here to Owl Shit. He deserves it for letting us in on that little family secret."

Happy tuck the glass over to the cell and handed it through the bars to Owl Shit, who grabbed on to it real eagerlike and slurped on it right away. "Thank you, Barjack," he said. Then he turned to Happy. "Say," he said, "is Happy your own real name?"

Happy kinda hung his head like as if he were ashamed a' something. "Yeah," he said, "it is."

"Your mama give it to you?"

"Yeah."

"How come her to call you that? Happy."

"Well, Owl Shit, whenever I final come on out, she were Happy."

"We could give you a nickname, Happy," said Churkee. "Something like, maybe, Gregory."

"Barjack," Happy said, "ain't it about time for me to relieve Butcher?"

"I reckon as how it is," I said, and he hurried on outta the jailhouse. Just as he slammed the door shut behint him, I heared a shot ring out. Churkee was the first one to the door, but I was close behint him.

"What was that?" Churkee called out.

Butcher come a-walking around the corner. "That was Happy shooting at a cowboy," he said. "I asked him, how come you to do that? And he said, Barjack's orders. If we see one a' Chugwater's men, we're s'posed to shoot him first and ask questions later. Is that right, Barjack?"

"That's what I said. You never heared me say it on account a' you was up on the roof."

"It was all right, then?"

"Damn right," I said. "Did Happy hit the son of a bitch?"

"I think he shot a hole in the cowboy's leg," said Butcher. "He howled and went a-hopping into the Hooch House."

"Maybe he'll bleed to death," I said. We all went back inside the marshaling office, and I went back behint my desk. I was a-looking out the hole in my front door what Pistol Polly had put there whenever she like to of kilt ole Dingle. I seen a flash across it from outside, and just in time I reckanized ole pettifogging Peester, the mayor a' Asininity. Pistol had raised that shotgun, and I yelled, "Don't shoot." She just had time to raise that barrel up as she pulled the trigger. The roar a' that scattergun inside the office like that damn near made my ears deaf, but I did hear Peester scream, and whenever the smoke cleared a little bit and I could see out the hole again, I didn't see him nowhere. I got up and run to the door and jerked it open to look out.

I seen Peester on his back in the dirt where he had fell off a' the boardwalk. "Peester," I said, "are you hurt?"

"Yes," he said. "I am. My butt is bruised." He reached over and picked up his silly little bowler hat and helt it up for me to look at. "And look. My hat is ruined." It did have little holes all in it.

"That ain't no loss," I said. "You can buy you a real one to replace it."

"What the hell was that all about?" he said, struggling to get up to his feet. "I might have been killed."

"I couldn't be that lucky, Your Orneriness," I said. "Get up and come on in."

I went on back to my chair behint my desk and set down. I tuck me a drink a' whiskey. Peester come huffing in then. "Why was I nearly killed?" he said.

"On account I hollered out a warning just in

time," I said. "If it weren't for that, you woulda been."

"You know what I mean," he said. His face was red, and he was a-trembling all over. "Why are you shooting at people through the front door of your office?"

"Oh, that," I said. "Well, I told ever'one who might be coming into the office to holler out their name before they went for the door. I guess I forgot to tell you. You see, we got a killer in jail here. It's Owl Shit Johnson. Ole Chugwater's baby brother, and Chugwater is a-trying to break him out. He's got the town plumb full a' his cowhands right now."

"Is that what all the shooting has been about?"

"Sure as hell. Are you just now getting around to asking about that?"

"Never mind that," he said. "I came down here to give you this telegram."

He helt out a piece a' paper toward me, but I never reached for it. I tuck another swaller a' my whiskey. "Read it to me," I said.

He looked more than a little put out, but he went and read it out loud anyhow. "The judge is detained in Frog Gulley. Stop. Will be in Asininity a week late. Stop. That's it."

I come up outta my chair real fast. "A week late," I roared. "Goddamn it. He can't do that to me. A week late." I picked up my glass and drained it down. Then I picked up the bottle and refilled the glass. I dropped back down into my chair real heavylike. Ever'body in the room come a-gethering around me.

"What's the matter with that, Barjack?" Peester said.

"That means we have to hold out here against Chugwater and his army for a whole damn two weeks," I said.

"Well," he said, "do your best," and he turned to head back out the door. "I'll be back when this entire unpleasantness is over with." He slammed the door behint him as he left.

"I wish you'da kilt him, Pistol," I said.

"It was you that stopped me," she said.

"Don't remind me."

"Barjack," said Churkee, "how are we going to hold out in here for another whole week? We haven't even got through the first week yet."

"We can do it," I said, not hardly believing my own words. "We'll have to go out and stock up on some stuff. Food. Ammunition. Tobacco."

"Some soap," said Polly.

"Okay," I said. "Ever'body think on what we'll need, and we'll make out a list."

We got the list all made out, and then Polly said, "Who's going to go out and fetch all that stuff?"

"I think you'll go," I answered her. "I don't think Chugwater and his boys'll shoot a gal."

"All right," she said. "Who'll set here with this shotgun?"

"Churkee," I said, and Churkee walked up to her and tuck the gun. She got up outta her chair and he set down in it. I scribbled out a note authorizing Polly to charge up all the stuff on the list at whatever store she had to go into to get it, and she tuck off. I settled back down to wait. I had put extry bottles a' whiskey on the list right at the top with a note to get it from the Hooch House, and I had put ceegars down and then I had put dynamite. A bunch a' sticks, and a box a' matches. I remembered how I had done near blowed up the whole town a-getting them Bensons that one time. I would do it again if it were called for.

By God, it weren't long before Bonnie come a-hollering at the front door, and we let her in, and she had some men with her a carrying a goddamn bathing tub. They set it down in the empty cell, and she sent them out to lug pails a' hot water in.

"What the hell is this all about?" I said.

"Polly said that some folks in here sure needed a bath," she said. "She had bought some soap, but said you needed a tub. Here's the soap. I brung it along."

"Where's Polly?" I said.

"She's still a-shopping," Bonnie said. "You give her a long list."

"It weren't all that long," I said.

"She had to stop at the Hooch House," Bonnie said, "and at the general store. I seen that list. It was long."

"All right," I said. "I guess it were."

I didn't want to get into no fight with Bonnie right there in front a' all a' my depitties and even ole Owl Shit, so I just agreed with her and shut the hell up. "Well, anyhow," I said, "I don't need that damn thing. I just had me a bath."

Bonnie looked over at me and smiled, a sickening, sweet smile, and I give her a grin in return.

"You can hang a blanket up on the bars there,"

she said, "and it'll be almost like having a private bathroom. Where you keep your blankets, Barjack?"

"In the back room," I said.

She waddled back there and come out in another minute with a stack a' blankets in her arms, and she went over to the cell and went to hanging them up. And by God, she was right. She damn near made a private bathroom right there in my jailhouse. Then she reached down between her great big tits and hauled out that bottle a' bubbly stuff and went and poured some in the water.

"Now," she said, stepping back out into the office, "I suggest that you nasty ole men wait till Miss Polly returns and let her use the water first. Then you can take your turns."

"They'll wait," I said.

"I had me a bath just a few weeks ago," Butcher said.

"You'll get another one today," said Bonnie.

Butcher looked at me with a kinda pleading look, and I looked back at him kinda sternlike and I nodded my head. Well, here come Polly, and she hollered out her name and come on in and put the stuff all on my desk. Bonnie told her that her bath was ready and showed her into the cell. Well, Polly were pretty damn thrilled. Then Bonnie tuck a chair and set her ass down on it right where someone coulda walked to take a peek around the blanket that was a-hanging there, and she pulled out her little Merwin Hulbert thirty-two caliber what I had got for her.

"The first man what walks over thissaway," she said, "is going to get shot."

Ever'one moved back the other way. Whenever Pistol Polly final got outta the tub and got herself dressed up again, she tuck the shotgun back from Churkee and told him to take a turn in the tub. He never had to be told twice. He went right in there, and then Bonnie and Polly went to fixing us up some good sandwiches with part a' what Polly had brung back from her shopping trip. She even tuck one in to Churkee so he could eat while he was in the water.

By and by, he come out and he was all dried and dressed. I looked at Butcher. "Harvey," I said, "I think it's your turn now."

"Aw, Barjack—"

"Go on," I said, and so he stomped his ass on into the cell behint the blankets.

"It ain't fair, you calling me that name when you won't even tell me what yours is," he yelled. I heared him splashing into the water.

"There ain't nothing wrong with Harvey," I said. "It's a perfect good name. I think I knowed someone else who was called by that name once. Harvey."

Chapter Seven

We all of us slept around in the jail that night except for either Happy or Butcher, one of which had to stay up on the roof at all times. I didn't want none of ole Chugwater's boys a-sneaking up on us, so I made 'em do that all night. It musta been somewheres around midnight when I and ever'one else was awoke rudely by a loud and raspy voice a-calling out, "Hey, in there. Don't shoot. Let me in. It's Bonnie." Well, I set up right quick and I seen Pistol Polly a-walking to the door to open it up. Bonnie come flouncing in, and Polly shut the door behint her and latched it again. I was on a cot in the extra cell, and I set up straight as a supporting pole for the roof overhang.

"Bonnie," I said, "what the hell are you a-doing here?"

She come a-running into the cell and grabbed me around with both a' her arms and squished me real damn good. "Barjack," she said, "I was worried about you and missing you something fierce."

"Hell," I said, "I'm okay over here. There weren't no need for you to come all the way down here like that."

"I want to stay here with you," she said, "just in case something was to happen."

"There ain't no need for that."

"Just in case some a' Chugwater's boys was to show up," she said. "I want to be with you."

I seen then that she was a-wearing, hanging over her shoulder, the gun belt I had give her with her thirty-two-caliber Merwin Hulbert in the holster. She meant to be ready for anything what might come up. I mean, that woman weren't a-skeered a' nothing a'tall. I couldn'ta done myself no better than have that there woman. She woulda tuck on a grizzler bear for me, I know it. She of a sudden pulled my face right toward her own and give me a big, sloppy smack on the lips. "I love you, Barjack," she said.

I kinda looked around to see that ever'one else had done dropped back off to sleep before I give her a answer, and then I said, "I love you too, sweet swaying hips." Then she laid me back down and undid my britches. "Bonnie," I said, "there's a mess a' folks in here."

"They're all asleep," she said, "and it's dark."

Then she hiked up her skirts and set right down on me and give me a hell of a romp right there in the jail cell. The blankets was still hanging up from the baths earlier, so I guess it was all right after all. When she was done with me, I needed me a drink a' brown whiskey.

"I'll fetch it for you, Barjack," she said. "I know where you keep it."

She paddle-footed outta the cell and on over to my desk, where she opened up the drawer and got out my bottle and a tumbler. She poured me a drink and brung it back into the cell and give it to me. I tuck me a big swaller right off. Then she tuck the glass back from me and had her own self a swig. I was glad to see her drinking right instead a' that pink swill she usual drunk. We finished off that glass in a hurry, and Bonnie tuck it back to my desk to refill it. By and by we snuggled down to sleep, and she mashed me up against the wall on that narrow little jail cell cot. I couldn't hardly breathe, I tell you.

Well, I guess it was about six or maybe seven when I final woked up, but I couldn't hardly see no way to get up off a' the cot without bothering Bonnie, and she sure as hell did not like to be bothered in the morning a'tall. In fact, that were the way I had learnt to fly that time. I had woked her up one morning and made her so mad she had picked me up by my collar and my belt and carried me out to the landing at the top a' the stairs in the Hooch House and flung me out into space over the saloon. And I had flow, I'm here to tell you. I didn't land none too good, but I had learnt to fly for sure.

Anyway, I wriggled around, but ever' way I tried I just got Bonnie's fat against me in some other way. I seemed to be helt down good. Well, I scruggled around till I got my ass set up at last, but my legs was still pinned down. I looked at her all snuggled down and sleeping peaceful-like, and I jerked my right leg up and out. I couldn't see no way out of it but to throw that leg over Bonnie, so I done it. Then I laid still for a spell to make sure that I hadn't woke her. She was still a-sawing logs. So I brung my other leg up and over. Then there weren't nothing for it but to pull myself up to where I was a-setting right on her and then to slide off on the far side, so I done that, but I done it real slow, and I never woked her up neither.

When I was final a-standing on dry ground with my two feet, I stood there real still and looked down at her for a spell. I couldn't see that I had disturbed her none a'tall. She were a deep sleeper, that's for sure. I picked up my tumbler from where we had dropped it and went out to my desk for a refill a' whiskey. I dranked it down in a record time a-setting back behint my desk. I think ever'one else in there was still fast asleep, and I never before in my life had heared such a cacophony a' snoring. (I learnt that there word from ole Dingle. I like to use it when I can.)

I stood up and farted a big fart, but it never woke up no one. I thunk about pouring out for myself another good glass full a' whiskey, but I never. Instead I went out the front door and looked over the mainest street of Asininity. It looked quiet all right. I didn't see no one out on the street. Course, it were early in the morning. The Hooch House was all closed up, I knowed. I walked out in the middle a' the street and looked up on the roof a' the jailhouse. I seen Happy a-setting up there looking out over the town and a-holding a Winchester rifle. "Happy," I called out to him

He looked down at me. "What, Barjack?"

"Is ever'thing as quiet as it looks to be?"

"Yes, sir."

"You ain't seen no cowhands come a-riding in from any direction?"

"Nary a one."

"Well, that's good," I said.

"Barjack?"

"What, ole pard?"

"Ain't my time about up here?"

"I reckon it is. I'll go chase out Butcher."

I went back inside after hollering out my name. When I stepped in, wasn't no one threatening me. I looked around the room, and I seen Butcher sprawled out on the floor a-snoring. I walked over to where he was at and give him a swift kick in the ass. He jumped up, real surprised. His eyes was real big. "What? What?" he said.

"I'd say it was about time you went up on top and spelled ole Happy for a while."

"Oh. Right. I'm on my way, Barjack."

He struggled on up to his feet, found his hat, and pulled it down tight. Then he headed out the front door. He was wearing his six-gun, but he didn't take no rifle with him. He would take the rifle Happy had up there. Whenever he went out, he slammed the door and woked up near ever'one else. They all went to moaning around and stretching and such. In another minute Happy come in, and he went right over to the coffeepot and commenced building a pot a' coffee. I don't rightly know just what it was that I had in my mind to do with myself, but the thought a' that coffee got to me in a big way. I wanted some real bad, so I just went back behint my desk and set down to wait.

It turned out to be a long wait, so I went and poured myself another whiskey. I was a-thinking about the big bad fight what was most likely coming our way. I recalled the big fights what I'd had in the past ever since I had become town marshal a' Asininity. I even thunk way back to the first big fight I'd had. The one with the damn Bensons. And it come to me that I had whipped them largely on account a' I had used dynamite. I had blowed their asses all over town. It come to me then that just in case it turned out to be real bad, I'd ought to have me some dynamite. "Happy," I said, "how long is it before that coffee is ready to be drunk?"

"Aw, I don't know, Barjack. It'll be a few minutes yet."

I got up and went back outside. I stopped for a minute on the boardwalk and looked up and down the street. It still looked clear. I walked on down to the hardware store and asked the ole bastard what run it if he had some dynamite. He did have, and so I told him I needed me about six sticks. He brought it out, and I tucked them into my inside coat pockets. "Send the goddamn bill to pettifoggin' Peester," I said, and I walked on out again.

I felt some better with that goddamn load of explosives all around my chest. Course, I also thunk that someone might get off a good shot at me and blow my ass all to hell. When I thunk that there thought, my steps got just a little bit longer and faster as I hurried my way back to the safety of my office. I sure as hell did not want to get scattered all over town thattaway. Whenever I got back I yelled out my name, and I went back inside and behint my desk. I pulled out a drawer and started unloading my pockets a' that stuff, stashing it all in my desk drawer.

"What's that, Barjack?" Butcher ast me.

"What the hell does it look like, moron?" I said. "Never mind about it nohow."

"Well, it looks like dynamite."

"Do tell," I said.

"What're you planning to do with it?"

"Didn't I tell you to never mind?"

"Well, yeah, you did."

"Then never mind it."

"All right. I don't mind it, but is it dynamite?"

"Butcher," I said, kinda like snapping at him.

He turned around and hung his head and sulked off in one a' the corners a' the room. I almost had a mind to explain things to him, but not quite. Bonnie come a-waddling out a' the cell from behint the hanging blankets just then, and she waddled right at me. I braced myself real good, and when she run into me, I stood my ground. I helt my breath whenever she give me her big bear hug too. "Good morning, Barjack," she said. "Ain't you glad I spent the night here with you?"

Whenever she turnt me a-loose, I said, "Yes, sweet tits, I sure as hell am."

"Can I pour you a tumbler a' your good whiskey?"

"No, I been a-waiting for that there coffee."

"It's damn near used up, Barjack," said Sly.

"I'll take the damn dregs," I said, and that's just

ezackly what I got too. The goddamn dregs. But I went right ahead and drunk them down, and then I went to spitting out bits a' coffee grounds. Bonnie put on a fresh pot for me. "Thanks, sweet tush," I said. Then it come to me that I'd have a few minutes' waiting time again, so I tole Bonnie to go on ahead and pour me a whiskey. She did too, and she give it to me. I dranked that down, and then by and by I final got my coffee. I was setting behint my desk a-sipping on it, and Sly come over and perched his ass on the desktop.

"Barjack," he said, "I don't know about you, but I would sure like to know what Chugwater is up to. I'd like to have a warning well before he comes back to town."

"Well, hell, Widdamaker," I said, "I would too, but I don't rightly know how we're going to get that warning. I've got either one a' Happy or Butcher on the roof a-watching. I don't know what more I can do."

"You can let me ride out to Chugwater's ranch and do a little spying," he said. "I think I could maybe find out something."

"Maybe get yourself kilt," I said.

"I've watched out for myself for a good many years now, and no one has killed me yet."

I slurped on my coffee and set the cup down. I looked up at him right into his steely eyes. "You really think you could might find something out?" I ast him.

"I think it would be worth a try," he said.

"When you want to go?"

"Right now."

"All right," I said. "Go on ahead, but be damn careful."

"You can count on that, Barjack," he said, and he left the office. I got up and walked to a front winder. Pretty soon I seen him riding by out in the street on his big black horse. It come back into my mind about the first time he come to town. He was already a well-knowed professional gun-fighting killer. It were widely knowed that he would kill a man, any man, for a price. So ever'one in town what had someone who was mad at him for some reason went to thinking that Sly had come to town to kill him. We had fights start and shootings take place and all kinds a' trouble over that. Ole Peester tried to get me to run him outta town, but I didn't have no reason to do that.

Me and Sly come to be good friends, and as it happened, he never come to town to kill no one. He were just taking a well-deserved rest. Then he went and fell for my goddamned ex-wife, and what was most likely worse, she fell for him, and they went and got theirselves hitched together. Me and Lillian had a kid, and Sly tuck that little devil too. Freed me up of all of them. That was the most luckiest thing that ever happened to me, I can tell you. Lillian had tried to kill me at least once, and shot a nick outta my ear. And the little shit just didn't have no respect for no one. Least of all for me. So I was sure as hell glad whenever Sly married up with my Lillian, I can tell you that much.

And I'll tell you even more about that widda-maker Sly. He were beyond a goddamn doubt the

fastest and more accurate and most coolest-
headedest gunfighter I have ever saw. I had done
been in a number a' scrapes with him by my side,
and there weren't no one in the world, not Wild-
ass Bill Hickok, not Wyatt Earp, not Ben Thomp-
son, not even that Black U.S. Marshal Bass Reeves,
not Bat Masterson, nor any of them big-name bastards, that I would ruther have had on my side
than that damn widdamaker, ole Sly. And I was
for sure glad when he decided that him and Lillian
would just stay settled right there in Asininity
where I could call on him for help whenever I
needed it real bad.

I tried not to bother him too much, but whenever things got real tough, I would ask him to
help out, and he never once refused me. No, sir.
And whenever I had his help, we always prevailed. (That there is another word I learnt from
ole Dingle, that "prevailed." It's a good one, don't
you think?) Anyhow, we killed ass on a number
a' gunfighting gangs, me and ole Sly, and that
there is the way we prevailed.

I didn't know what the hell he was a-planning
on doing out at Chugwater's ranch, but whatever
the hell it was, I figgered he would damn well get
it did. I had Bonnie pour me out another cup a'
coffee. It were good coffee. And while I was slurp-
ing at it, Dingle come over to my desk. "Barjack,"
he said, "what is Sly up to?"

"I ain't for sure, Scribbler," I said. "He's got him
some idee about spying up on ole Chugwater. I
don't know ezackly what he's going to do, but he'll
do something, don't you never worry none about

that. Whenever Sly gets something on his mind, he's a-going to pull it off. I can promise you that much."

"Okay," he said. "Thanks, Barjack."

And he went back over to his chair in the corner and went to scribbling some more in his notebook. I figgered that what we was into just right at that goddamn minute was already going into another a' them dime novels about me what Dingle had been writing now for quite a spell. Me and him both was a-getting rich off a' them things. To tell you the truth, I was a-worrying about ole Sly my own self. Hell, it was broad daylight. How the hell was he a-going to ride out to Chugwater's ranch and find out anything? I couldn't see it. He damn sure wouldn't be able to sneak up to the house and listen at a winder. Someone would see him for sure. Someone would plug him with a bullet. As good a gunman as he was, he weren't no match for a whole army a' cowhands. And just then a horrible thought come into my head.

What if ole Sly was to get hisself kilt? What would ole Lillian do then? Would she come back after me? Would I get my ass stuck again with her and that goddamn snotty kid? It was enough to make me sick to my stomach, and I went and poured myself another glass full a' good brown whiskey.

Chapter Eight

Well, I was a-setting there worrying my ass off about ole Sly getting hisself foolishly kilt out there at Chugwater's ranch and thinking that I had been a fool to agree to his going out there. I wisht I had rid with him too. I coulda stopped him from doing any goddamn foolish bullshit what was too damn dangerous. I poured myself another glass a' whiskey, and Bonnie seen me. She come a-waddling over to the desk. "Barjack, I coulda done that for you, sweetie. Whyn't you call me?"

"I can pour a goddamn glass a' whiskey," I said.

Sly come back final. He had been gone for quite a spell, and the rest a' my gang was getting mighty restless, I can tell you. They was wanting some action. Once ole Butcher had piped up and said, "Why don't we just ride out to that damn Chugwater's place and attack the bastards? Why do we have to sit around here and wait for him?"

"Butcher," I said, "I am the town marshal a' this here town. I ain't got no jurisprudence outside a' town. We'd just be a bunch of owl hoots attacking a man's ranch if we was to do that. What we're a-doing here is we're guarding the jail and our prisoner. We just has got to keep our patience. That's all."

And he weren't the only one neither. They was all getting kinda jumpy. Me too, but I never let on so they could tell it. So I was damn glad whenever Sly final come back. I even jumped up from my chair and practical run across the room to meet him, but so did ever'one else, and I run smack into Bonnie and fell over back'ards and landed on my ass. "Barjack, I'm sorry," she said, and she helped me up to my feet. Ever'one was talking all at the same time and asking Sly what he had found out, so I at last yelled out for them all to shut up. They did. Then I stepped right up to Sly and looked him in the face.

"What'd you find out?" I said.

"They'll be coming in in the morning," he said. "And Chugwater's called in another twenty men. They mean to attack with a full force and kill us all if that's what it takes to free Owl Shit."

"By God," I said, "we'll be a-waiting for them."

"That's not all," he said.

"What more?"

"He means to block off the town so we can't get out. Both ends. He's sending men in right now to do that."

I scratched my head, walking back to my chair. "What the hell would we want to get outta town for?" I said. "We're guarding this here jail."

"Chugwater thought that you might think to ride over to the county seat and ask Sheriff Cody for some help."

I thunk hard for a minute till it got to hurting

my head, and then I said, "I wonder how in the hell he come up with that. That's just ezackly what I was a-thinking about doing. Butcher, go back up on the roof and send Happy down here."

"Yes, sir." And Butcher run outside. I was thinking to send Happy, but I thunk better a' it before he come in. I decided that I would ride over to the county seat my own self and get that damned Cody and make him help out. I knowed that I would be more persuasive than what Happy could be. I checked my Merwin Hulbert self-extracting revolver, and then I went over to the gun rack to get me a good rifle. I picked out a good Henry what I liked. Happy come in the door just then.

"Happy," I said, "I'm leaving you in charge here. You know what to do."

"Where you going, Barjack?" he ast me.

"I'm riding over to see Cody," I said. "I'll be back quick as a flash. In the meantime, you take care a' things around here. Ask Sly to tell you what he found out."

I stuck a bottle a' whiskey down into my coat pocket. Bonnie run up and grabbed on to me. "Barjack, be careful," she said.

"Don't worry, sweet hips," I told her.

"Barjack," said Sly, "are you sober enough for this?"

"I'll be all right."

I walked on out and then down the street to the stable, where I got me my favorite horse and had the man saddle him up for me. And I tell you what. I did stagger some in my walking. Even so, while I was a-waiting for my horse to get saddled,

I pulled out my bottle and had me a snort. Then I tuck out a ceegar and lit it up with a match I had in my pocket. My horse was ready, and I climbed into the saddle. It were a bit difficult, but I made it, and then I rid outta there and headed for the county seat.

I rid as fast as I dared to ride, and once I nearly wobbled outta the saddle. That shook me up some, so I slowed down a bit and set more careful in the saddle. I got outta town and was a-riding alongside a' the big clump a' rocks what set beside a' the road out there, when I seen a gang a' five men riding toward me. I turned and went behint them rocks. I dismounted and tuck my Henry with me. Laying that rifle acrost a rock, I cranked a shell into the chamber. The riders come to a halt out there in the road.

"Barjack," one a' them called out.

"It's me," I answered.

"You might just as well get back on that horse and ride back into town," he said. "No one's getting out."

"You bastards think you can stop me," I said, "you just come right on ahead and try."

He laughed. "You're already stopped," he said. "You ain't going no farther."

I tuck my Henry in my left hand and reached inside my coat with my right to find a stick a' dynamite, which I brung out. I helt the fuse to my ceegar tip till it begun to fizzle, and then I helt it a little bit longer. Final, I stood up behint that rock and heaved that son of a bitch just as hard as I could. It went a-flying up and out and landed in the road just in front a' the five a' them.

"Hey," yelled one.

"Goddamn," said another one.

The rest a' them mighta been thinking about hollering out something, but they never got no chance. That there dynamite blew, and it blew big. It scattered pieces a' horses and men all over the road, along with dirt and rocks and sticks and such. I looked around and didn't see no survivors. I pulled out my bottle and tuck me another drink. Then I walked back to my horse and put a foot in a stirrup. I grabbed on to the saddle horn and went to swing my right leg over the horse, but I lost my balance and fell down in the dirt. "Goddamn it," I said.

I struggled around till I was on my hands and knees, and then I reached up with a hand for the stirrup. The horse was kinda dancing around, and he dragged me in a circle kinda. "Whoa. Whoa, you son of a bitch," I said. Final he settled down some, and I managed to pull myself back up onto my feet. Then I got on his back, but it weren't no easy task.

I had to ride real careful acrost that place in the road to keep from riding right through some sloppy mess what I had made there. Even so my ole nag stepped right on a piece a' arm what was right in the middle a' the road. It made me kinda wince. "Damn fools," I said, "think you can hold me up." The rest a' the way over to the county seat I was thinking about that damned Chugwater and what I would like to do to him whenever I got me the chance to do it. I pulled out my bottle now and then and had me a swig a' that good stuff.

I was feeling pretty damn high by the time I pulled up in front a' Cody's office. I just set there in the saddle for a bit. Final I dragged my ass outta the seat and stepped down onto the street. My legs buckled and I like to set down, but I never. I kept on my feet. I turned real slow and deliberate and tied my ole horse to the rail. Then I aimed myself at the door to Cody's office and walked up there, stumbling a bit on the step up to the boardwalk. I got to the door and grabbed on to the handle, but the goddamn door was locked. I pounded on it before I decided that Cody just weren't there.

Then I figgered the lazy bastard was acrost the street at the saloon what was over there. I pulled myself up straight and headed for it. I weaved my way clean acrost the street, dodging one wagon and two horses that come along, but I final made it over there. I shoved the batwing doors open and stepped in. The doors hit me in the ass. I stood looking around till I spotted Cody, and then I went to walking straight at him. He was a-setting at a round table in a front corner a' the bar. He looked up when he seen my mass a-coming, and then he stood up. "Barjack," he said. "What brings you over this way?"

"I got problems in Asininity, Cody," I said. "I need your help."

"Sit down, Barjack," he said, "and tell me about it. You want a drink? You don't look like you need one."

"Hell, yes, I want a drink," I said. Cody called for a whiskey, and they brung it to me, in a little sissy glass. "I'm more serious than this," I said, so the barkeep went and brung back a good-sized glass and set it down in front a' me. He stood there a-waiting till Cody said, "Put it on my tab." Then he went away. First thing I done was to drink down that first little sissy drink he brung me.

"All right, Barjack," Cody said. "What's your problem?"

They was other men a-setting at that table with Cody, but he never bothered to interduce none a' them. I done like he done. I just ignored them.

"I arrested Owl Shit the other day for a killing he done in the Hooch House," I said. "His brother, ole Chugwater, has swore to get him out. I got all my depitties guarding the jailhouse waiting for the judge to get to town. Chugwater has called in twenty gunslingers to help him. He's blocked off Asininity too. I need you and a good-sized posse to ride over to Asininity to help us out."

Cody tuck a swig a' his drink. Then, "Barjack," he said, "you've been in scrapes bigger than this before, and you always got yourself out all right. Why do you think you need my help this time?"

"Hell, Cody," I said, "Chugwater had twenty cowhands to begin with. Now he's got forty men. I ain't got but maybe six depitties, and one of them's a scribbler and two of them's women. You're the goddamn county sheriff, and Asininity's in your county. It's your damn job."

"I don't know, Barjack."

"They tried to stop me from riding over here," I

said. "Five of them, but I blowed their asses all to hell."

"Then there's only thirty-five left," he said. "Barjack, you don't need me."

"What the hell kind of a lawman are you anyway?" I said. He was beginning to piss me off. "Hell. You know what I think? I think you ain't even really related to ole Buffalo Bill Cody a'tall. I think your real name ain't even Cody. That's what I think."

Cody stood up. "You trying to start something with me?" he said.

"If I do start anything with you, I'll finish it too," I said.

He set back down. "Barjack, you're drunk. I don't know if I can believe anything you've said to me."

"Goddamn it, Cody," I said, "it's all true. I've got Owl Shit in my jail cell, and I've got Happy and Butcher there a-watching. And then I've got Dingle and Sly and the Churkee and Pistol Polly and my big fat Bonnie. And Chugwater's riding in first thing in the morning with sixty men intending to kill them all. Me too, if I'm back in time."

"Why don't you get you a room and sleep it off?" Cody said. "We'll talk about it some more when you're sober."

"I ain't got time to sleep," I said. "I got to get back to my gang. They're going to need ever' gun they can get."

"Hell, you couldn't hit the street right now, the shape you're in."

I jerked out my Merwin Hulbert right fast and tuck a shot what nicked his left earlobe. The blood went to rushing down his neck and onto his shirt. He screamed, grabbed his ear, and jumped up to his feet.

"Goddamn you, Barjack."

"How's that for shooting?" I said.

"You drunken son of a bitch." He looked up at me and kinda nodded like, but he weren't nodding at me, I figgered out later. He were nodding at some son of a bitch what was standing right behind me. Something crashed down on top a' my head, and the whole world went black as a dark night out on the prairie when the stars is blanked out by dark clouds. Only in a minute I seen the stars anyhow. Then I fell over, and I don't know nothing else about that night. I woked up the next morning laying on a cot in a jail cell. I moaned and rolled my head and seen that the door was closed.

I thunk things through, and it come to me that right at that very minute my friends back in Asininity might could be in one big gunfight with Chugwater's damn bunch. Hell, some a' them might even be kilt already. I set up on the edge a' the cot and screamed, "Cody. Goddamn you. Let me outta here."

I didn't get no answer. I screamed his name out another time or two. Still nothing. Damn, I was worried about Happy and Butcher and Sly and Bonnie and Polly and Churkee. I was even worried about ole Dingle some little bit. I wondered if he would ever get to write the book he was messing with. I stood up and looked down at my holster and seen that my Merwin Hulbert weren't there. That goddamn son of a bitching Cody had swiped it. I walked over to the door and tried it. Sure enough, it was locked. I grabbed on to two bars and rattled the shit outta that door. Still no one come around.

There was a bucket over in a corner, and I went and pissed in it. Then I picked it up and walked over to the door a' the cell. I looked out at Cody's desk and I swung that bucket and slung its contents as hard as I could. They slopped over the floor and over the top a' the desk. Then I put it back where it come from. I heard a key in the front door, and I went back to the cot and laid my ass back down, pretending to still be asleep. Someone come in. I rolled my head over and opened a eye to peek out, and I seen that it was Cody's depitty. I set up.

"Hey, Buffalo Bill, Junior," I called out.

"You talking to me?" he said.

"Ain't you Cody's kid?"

"I'm his deputy."

"Then get the damn keys and let me outta here."

"I can't do that, Marshal," he said. "Sheriff Cody's the one that put you in here, and he'll have to let you out. If he decides to let you out. You like to have shot off his ear last night."

"I shoulda shot off his damn head," I said.

"Then for sure you'da never got out."

"Look, Junior, I got problems over in Asininity. I got to get back there."

"Ain't nothing I can do."

"Well, get me some coffee at least," I said.

He started to walk to the coffeepot, and he stepped in a puddle a' piss on the floor and his foot went a-shooting out ahead a' him, and he landed right on his ass, right in that puddle a' piss. He yelped like he had been shot.

"What's wrong, Junior?" I said.

"Goddamn it, Barjack," he said, "did you do that?"

"What?"

"Piss all over the floor?"

"Is that piss?" I said, real innocent-like.

"It sure does smell like piss."

"I wish I could piss that far," I said. "By God, I'd do it all the time just for the fun a' it."

Chapter Nine

Well, Junior was still a-mopping up the floor whenever ole Cody come in at last. I jumped up and
yelled at him. "Cody, goddamn it, let me outta
here. All kinds a' shit is a-fixing to bust loose over
at Asininity. I'm needed. Open this damn door."

"Keep your pants on, Barjack," he said. "I'd
ought to keep you in there for six weeks at least
after what you done. Drunk and disorderly, assaulting a peace officer. Shit, if I was to hold you
for trial, you might never get out of prison."

All the time he was a-talking, he was picking
up his damn keys and walking to the cell. He unlocked the door. Then he walked back over to his
desk and opened up a drawer. He pulled my
trusty Merwin Hulbert outta the drawer. I didn't
waste no time. I was right behint him. He turned
around and handed me that gun, and I dropped
it in my holster.

"Where's my goddamn horse?" I said.

"Right outside at the hitching rail."

"I guess you ain't a-going to give me no help?"

"Not a damn bit," Cody said, "and I hope they
kill you before it's over with."

"That ain't a very neighborly thought," I said as I tramped across the room to the front door. I jerked the door open and went outside, and then I slammed the door real hard, hoping that I'd break the glass in the winder, but I never. There was my horse just like he'd said. I went down to it and untied it. Then I clumb up on his back and turned it to ride outta town back toward Asininity. I rid hard and fast outta town just for show. I knowed I wouldn't be able to ride like that all the way back, but I wanted them to see what a desperate hurry I was in. Soon as I got outta town and outta sight, I slowed my ole nag to a halt.

I rid along that way for a spell before I whipped him up again. I didn't see no one on the road, and I had made it just about halfway home. I decided that the ole horse needed a rest, so I stopped and got off and let him graze and drink from the stream what run alongside a' the road. I found me a whiskey bottle in my saddlebags, and I tuck it out for a drink. I tell you what, I felt some better after a few slugs a' that wonderful stuff. I caught up my nag and remounted and continued on my way.

When I final come to that big rock just outside a' my town, I seen that the bodies I had left there was gone. Someone had come along and cleaned up after me. It had to 'a' been some a' Chugwater's bunch. I thunk it over real careful and couldn't come up with no one else who might coulda done it. Then it come to me, if Chugwater knowed that his boys was kilt, then he'da put some more there. I squinnied my eyes around and couldn't see no sign a' no cowboys hanging around, but they coulda been hid behint that big rock pile just the same as what I had been. I decided it would be foolhardy a' me to just go riding past that place.

There weren't no other road going into town from that side a' town, so I rid off the road and across the prairie. If there was some one behint the rocks, they never seen me. It tuck a little time, but I final come into town from the backside, and when I got close, I could hear gunshots. It sounded like a small war going on. I knowed that Chugwater had laid siege to the jailhouse, and I figgered that all a' my men and women was on the inside a' the jail. Well, maybe Happy or Butcher was on the roof, if they hadn'ta picked him off from down below.

There was a little slip a' the Chugwater River what run past the backside a' the town, and I had to ride through it. It didn't hardly deserve the name a' river, though. I coulda jumped across it. Well, I coulda, a few years ago. I wondered as I slopped across if ole Chugwater had been named for the river or if the river had been named after him. I had been in Asininity for a few years by this time, and both a' them had been around for a time before I come along. I guessed it didn't make a shit, though. There was a little bridge down a little farther I coulda crossed over, but I didn't want to ride down that far. It went over to a abandoned mill. The gunshots got louder as I went in closer.

I was worrying about had any a' my people got

shot, and I was anxious to get back to the jail, but I needed to do it without getting my own ass kilt. So what I done was I rid into the stable through the back door, and I give my horse to that man. Then I drawed my Merwin Hulbert and went to the big front door. Leaning against the doorjamb, I peeked out, and I could see cowboys all over the damn place. They was all a-shooting toward the jail. I remember thinking, I could pick off one or two of them easy, maybe more, but there was so damn many a' them that I couldn't figger what good that would do. It would just alert them to my own whereabouts, and I didn't need that.

Then the gunshots got hot and heavy, and I decided I could get at least one a' the bastards and no one would notice the shot. I tuck a bead on one. He was real busy aiming and shooting at the jail. I drilled him right betwixt his shoulder blades, and he dropped like a sack. Then I went to running back through the stable. As I passed the stable man, I said, "You ain't seen me. You ain't seen nothing. If you say anything to anyone, I'll do you like I just done that son of a bitch out there."

"I don't know nothing, Barjack," he said. "I ain't seen you all day."

I went back out his back door and sneaked along the backsides a' the buildings. When at last I come to the backside a' the jailhouse, I was relieved that none a' the cowboys was back there. I walked past the ladder what Happy and Butcher had been a-using to get up on the roof, and I jerked open the back door and screamed, "Don't shoot. It's Barjack." Then I went on in fast and slammed the door behint me. "What dumb son of a bitch went and left the back door unlocked?" I said, and I latched it shut. Bonnie come a-running and damn near knocked me over when she grabbed me in her bear hug. "Barjack," she said, "I was so worried when you never come back."

"Well, I'm back, and I ain't hurt," I said. Happy come over then, and he said, "How many men is Cody sending?"

"He ain't sending no one," I tole him, "the chicken shit."

"There's too many of them out there, Barjack," he said.

"Where are they located?" I ast him. "Is they all scattered or is they in a bunch somewheres?"

"They're all over town," he said, "but there is a bunch of them just about across the street."

"Is anyone in here hurt?"

"No, we're all okay."

"Good," I said. I reached under my coat and pulled out a stick a' dynamite and held it out to Happy. I knowed that he had a good throwing arm. "Light you up a smoke," I said. "Then go out back and climb up on the roof. Keep down so no one will spot you. Move up to the front a' the building, and touch your ceegar to this here fuse. Then toss the son of a bitch right smack in the middle a' that bunch acrost the street. That should oughtta narrow the odds down a bit."

"Barjack," he said, his eyes wide-open, "is that fair?"

"What the hell do you mean? Who gives a shit? Just do it."

"Yes, sir," he said.

I left him to do what he'd been tole to do and walked up to the front a' the jailhouse. Everyone was a-shooting out the winders and the Churkee was a-shooting through that hole in the front door.

"Are you'ns narrowing the odds any?" I said, pulling out my Merwin Hulbert.

"A little," said Sly.

"Well, we'll narrow them considerable more in a minute."

I tuck me a peek out the winder and seen that bunch acrost the street. There was maybe eight or ten a' them, and they was all hunkered down behint barrels and boxes a' stuff and shooting at my winders. I was a-thinking, You goddamn assholes are in for a big surprise. I heared Happy's footsteps over my head, and I added, Right about now. Then I seen that dynamite come a-flying, its fuse a-sparkling, and it lit right snug up against one a' the barrels them bastards was a-hiding behint.

"What's that?" said Bonnie.

"It's a blow-them-all-to-hell stick," I said. "Just watch."

Just then it blowed, and I seen men and pieces a' men and bits a' barrels and parts a' the storefront all a-flying all over the street, and there was a ringing in my ears what I thunk wouldn't never stop. There was screaming outside too and shouting. It was like a scene from behint the gates a' hell, or at least it was like a battle in a war.

"Who done that?" said Bonnie.

"Happy done it just like I tole him to do," I said.

Gradual things settled down outside after the last stick had dropped outta the sky. It was real quietlike. In another minute or so, Happy come in again through the back door. "How'd I do, Barjack?" he said.

"You done just fine," I said. "You blowed their ass up."

Sly said, "They're mounting up and riding out."

"The ones that're left," Churkee added.

"We won?" said Happy.

"This round," I said.

"They'll be back," said Sly.

I unlatched the front door and opened it. Then I stepped out onto the boardwalk and Sly follered me. We was each still a-holding our six-guns in our hand, and we looked up and down the street. It seemed like the cowboys was all gone for sure. "I think things'll be quiet around here for a while now," Sly said.

"I expect you're right about that," I said.

"The only thing is," he said, "Chugwater's down to about half the number of gunmen he had now."

"He'll be a little easier to deal with."

"Maybe. He'll be more desperate."

"Yeah, I reckon you're right about that too."

"We'll just have to act like we're more desperate too."

"We will," I said.

Just then a cowboy came riding hard down the street. Me and Sly was both some relaxed, and I damn sure weren't ready for him to throw down on me with a six-gun as he rid past real fast. He fired a shot and it nicked me right where my neck growed outta my shoulder on the right side. I yelped and grabbed at it with my left hand. I staggered back and leaned against the wall. Sly made out to shoot back, but before he could get off a shot, a rifle barrel sticking out of a winder fired, and that cowboy went a-tumbling off a' his horse.

I staggered inside and went into the free cell and fell down on the cot. I was bleeding something ferocious. Bonnie seen it and went to screaming. Sly said, "I'll get the doc," and went running off. "Somebody get me some whiskey," I said.

Bonnie dropped down on her fat knees right beside a' me and went to wringing my free hand. "Barjack," she said, "Barjack. Don't die on me. Sly went after Doc."

Polly brung in my whiskey bottle from the desk, and I pulled my hand a-loose from Bonnie's grip and tuck it. I had me a long drink. Then I said, "Hell, I ain't going to die. I'm too damn pissed off to die."

"Does it hurt, Barjack?" Bonnie said.

"It hurts like hell," I said. "Who shot that son of a bitch?"

"I did," said Polly.

"Do you reckon it was worth it to him to'a nicked me and then got his ass kilt like that?" I said.

Bonnie tore off a piece a' her petticoat and pulled my left hand away from the wound. Then she went to daubing at it with that rag. She made a hell of a face while she was a-doing that.

"Does it look that bad?" I said.

"It looks pretty damn bad," she said. "Polly, bring me some water, will you?"

"Sure," Polly said, and in another minute she done it. Bonnie dipped that rag in the water and daubed a little bit more. Then she tuck my left hand and washed the blood off a' it. She tore off another bit a' rag off a' her petticoat and folded it up and laid it on that wound and held it down tight. About then the doc come in. Someone pointed him to the cell and Bonnie got outta his way.

He studied on my hurt neck for a little bit, and then he went to messing with it. Whenever he was all done, I had some kinda salve rubbed on it and a bandage tied down on it. He stood up and picked up his bag. "Just keep quiet," he said. "Don't do anything strenuous for a while. It'll heal up."

"Send your bill to Peester," I said. He walked on out.

I drank me some more whiskey outta my bottle, and pretty soon I dropped off to sleep. I dreamt that someone had shot me, and my whole head went flying off. I don't know how I coulda been conscious the whole time and even seen my own head rolling around in the street, but that was the way it was. Course, it was only a dream. But whenever I woked up I couldn't help thinking how stupid it was. Hell, my eyeballs was out there in my goddamn head, and it was rolling around in the street along with them other pieces a' men what Happy had blowed up. I was a-standing on the boardwalk without no head, and so a' course, without no eyes, but still I was a-looking at my own head out there. Dreams can be awful damn dumb sometimes. Dingle had called that some kinda word one time, and I was a-wishing I could remember that word, but it just wouldn't come to me.

I tried to turn my head, but it hurt too bad to do that, so I just yelled out, "Dingle. You out there?" He come into the cell right quick, and he looked like he had been in a war. His shirttail was out on one side, and his shirt was full a' bullet holes. There wasn't no blood, though. His hair was all messed up, and his face and his shirt was smudged black from the powder his own shots had blowed back on him. "Damn," I said when I seen him. He kinda grinned. He was holding his pad and a pencil, though.

"They came close but they never hit me," he said. "What did you want with me, Barjack?"

"What was that there word you used once? You said it meant something what was like a dream. Do you recollect?"

"Oh," he said. "Yeah. It was surreal."

"Surreal," I said. "Surreal. Yeah. That's it. Well, I just had me a surreal dream. My head was shot off, and I was a-looking at it. It was a surreal son of a bitch."

"Yeah. It sounds like it."

"So that there's the right word for it?"

"I'd say so," said Dingle. "It sure sounds surreal to me."

"Surreal," I said, and I said it over and over on account a' I wanted to remember it. I liked getting new words from Dingle. That was half the fun a' keeping him around, although it weren't bad to make money off a' him and his books, the ones what he writ about me and my adventures. I figgered he was a-working on another one right then.

Then I decided that we was all of us in the middle of a goddamned surreal situation. There was Owl Shit in jail for doing a dumb killing, and his dumb brother, Chugwater, trying like hell to bust him out. Then there was pieces a' dead men all over the street. It was all pretty damn surreal as far as I could tell.

Chapter Ten

Well, nothing much happened for the next couple a' days, and it was a damn good thing too, on account a' my neck begun to hurt like hell. I had been shot before, a' course, but it never did hurt me like that goddamn nick in my neck hurt. I couldn't think a' nothing for a time except only that I wanted a drink a' good whiskey, and I had me a good many a' those. The guys and gals all hung around the jailhouse and kept a watch out for any a' Chugwater's bunch what might show up, but none of them did. I final got to thinking about the mess we was in, and the first thing I thunk about was why in the hell I was so damn determined to hang on to that damned Owl Shit. I couldn't come up with nothing. He sure as hell weren't worth me getting my own self or any a' my friends and 'special my sweet Bonnie big tits kilt over. So why in the hell didn't I just let ole Chugwater have the little shit? I couldn't hardly answer that damn nagging question.

I sure weren't one for upholding the dignity a' my office at all costs. No, sir. I didn't have no such

scruples, so it weren't that. Were it my own personal pride and puffed-upness? The little asshole
had shot a man dead right in front a' me and a
dozen or two witnesses. I had to hold him in jail
to keep the respect a' all the folks in town. If I was
to let a goddamn murderous bastard like that just
walk away, why, they'd all just commence to doing whatever the hell it was they wanted to do,
thumbing their noses at me. I couldn't have that.
Maybe that was the reason. Maybe.

Then it come to me that ole Dingle had been
a-writing all them books about me, about what a
goddamn staunch upholder a' the law I was and
how I could handle any damn situation. It come
to me that maybe I was a-trying to live up to the
image what Dingle had created. They was a whole
bunch a' people out there somewheres a-reading
them books. Well, hell, whatever. The whole truth
a' the matter was that I just for damn sure meant
to hold on to Owl Shit for as long as it was nec-
essary. I weren't about to give in to Chugwater.
No way.

Bonnie come into the cell where I was a-laying
and drinking and thinking. She set down on the
cot beside a' me, even though there was barely
room for her fat ass. She just kinda perched one
cheek on the cot. It musta been a kind a' strain on
her to set thattaway, but she done it on account a'
she loved my ass so much. She petted on me and
cooed around and called me sweet names and
tole me how proud a' me she was and how much
she was a-wishing that I'd get to feeling a whole

lot better real damn soon. I surely did enjoy that too, I can tell you.

I seen Happy out in the office walk over to the coffeepot for a cup a' the hot stuff, and I yelled out at him. "Happy, is Butcher up on the roof?"

"Yes, sir, he is."

"Good," I said. Happy come a-walking into the cell.

"Barjack," he said, "do you think we need to keep this up?"

"This what?" I ast him.

"You know. Keeping us all in here all the time. Chugwater's men ain't been around for a few days. Maybe he's give it up."

"Don't you believe that for a minute, Happy," I said. "A man like Chugwater don't quit. Not never. He won't quit till Owl Shit's hanged up or till him or me is dead. He lives by a code, and that code is don't quit."

"But we've killed a bunch a' his men."

"And he promised his mama that he'd take care a' his little brother," I said, "and that's another part a' the code. Mind your mama. Respect your mama. And keep your word. That's all a part a' it. He'll be back. Don't you fret about that. He'll be back, and he'll be meaner than ever."

"Yes, sir," said Happy. "Well, I guess I had better get up on the roof and relieve Butcher." He walked on out and left me and Bonnie there to pet on each other. Course, she had never quit petting on me while he was there talking to me. That woman didn't have no sense a' shame a'tall.

I got to thinking about what I had tole Happy about Chugwater being devoted to his mama and to protecting his little brother. I wondered for a minute what I would do in his situation. I couldn't hardly remember my mama nor any a' my brothers. But what if, before I had run away from New York, what if my mama had made me to promise to take care a' one a' my brothers, or all a' them? And what if, after that, my brother had wound up in jail charged with a killing? What the hell would I have did? I thunk about that for about a minute, and I concluded then that I would let the little shit hang, and I would let my mama curse me for it. I believe I could walk around and function just fine with a curse on my head.

I realized right then that I was getting to kinda admire ole Chugwater, even though I would never have did what he was a-doing. He was standing up against all odds, meaning the law, for what he believed in. He was out to save his little brother, even though the little brother were a little snivelly shit-ass. He weren't afraid a' nothing, that Chugwater. Hell, I had me a mean-ass reputation, and he weren't about to back down from me. And then there was ole Sly, the goddamn widdamaker. Sly had kilt no one knows how many men, and all in fair fights too. He was knowed and feared far and wide, and Chugwater was standing against both a' us. You just had to admire that.

At the same time that I was admiring the bastard, I was thinking about how it would feel to shoot the son of a bitch to death. Just then I couldn't think a' nothing that would make me feel quite as good as killing ole Chugwater and then watching his little brother hang. I really had it in for the two a' them. They had caused me a whole world a' trouble, and then went and got me shot in the neck, and it was hurting me pretty damn bad, I can tell you. I didn't let on to no one other than my Bonnie that I was hurting so bad, though. I only let on to her on account a' she was taking so much pity on me and petting me up so much.

"How are you doing, Barjack?"

I jerked my head up to see who it was had snuck in on me like that, and it hurt me when I did, but then I seen that it were ole Sly. "Goddamn it, Sly," I said. "You surprised the hell outta me."

"Sorry, pard," he said.

"Oh, hell," I said, "I'm a-doing all right, considering that I damn near got my head shot off. I'll be up and at 'em again in no time."

"I'm glad to hear it," he said.

Just then the doc come in, and Sly excused hisself and went back out into the office. Whenever Doc come over to the cot, Bonnie struggled up to her feet and moved over to one side. Doc bent over me and pulled the bandage off a' my neck, and I hollered when he done that. He poked around on it for a bit, and then he said, "Well, it's healing up nicely." He turned to Bonnie and said, "Just keep him quiet for a little longer. I'll look back in on him in another couple of days." He left then and Bonnie set her half a' her ass back on the cot. She smiled down at me real simpering sweetlike.

"He said it's healing up nicely," she said.

"I heared what he said."

"Ain't you glad of it?"

"Hell, yeah, I'm glad. I don't like laying here and hurting like this."

"Well, it won't be for much longer, sweetie."

I was a-wishing that the day would hurry up and go by and get to nighttime, so I could have her pull them blankets and rags tight around us and shut out the rest a' the world. I was getting a sudden urge to have me a romp with my sweet tits, but I never said nothing about it to her. Whenever she leaned over me, though, it looked to me like them big tits was just about to jump outta their sacks right into my face. Lordy, they was big and fine.

Butcher poked his nose into the cell just then. "Barjack," he said, "four cowboys just come a-riding into town."

I set up on the cot real quicklike. "Is they Chugwater's men?" I ast him.

"I ain't for sure."

"Well, where did they go?"

"They pulled up in front a' the Hooch House."

"Find out who they are," I said.

"Okay." He disappeared again, and pretty soon I thunk I could hear him climbing up onto the roof. In another minute he come back down, and in another minute after that, he were back in the cell. "Happy said they was Chugwater's men," he tole me.

"Just four a' them?" I said.

"That's all I seen."

"Well, stay alert. Keep an eye out for them. As long as they're in the Hooch House a-spending money, it's all right."

If they was a-spending money in the Hooch House, that meant that I was a-making money. I hoped that they would stay in there and spend till they was broke. Course, they could get more money real easy just by killing me, but I didn't intend that they would do that. Butcher come back in.

"Four more come in," he said. "They went in the Hooch House too."

"All right," I said. "Just keep a-watching. Butcher."

"Yes, sir."

"Does Sly know about them?"

"Yes, sir. I told him."

"Okay. That's good."

"Barjack," said Bonnie, "you know what Doc said. Lay back down. You need to relax and get some rest."

She pushed me back down onto my back, but I struggled right back up. "Hell, that's all I been do-ing is resting," I said. "I can at least set up, can't I?"

"Well, all right, if you'll set still."

"I'm a-setting still," I said.

She scooted around till her whole entire ass was on the cot, and she was a-setting right beside a' me. She wrapped a big arm around my shoulders and pulled me into her.

"Ow," I said.

"What's the matter, dearie?" she said. "Did I hurt you?"

"You pinched my hurt neck some," I tole her.

She loosened up her vise grip a little then, but she kept her arm around me. "I'm sorry, sweetie," she said, and she give me a slobbery kiss on the cheek. "I didn't mean to hurt you."

"Hell," I said, "that's all right."

I could see out into the office some by then, mostly the front wall and winders, and I could see that Sly and Butcher and Polly and Churkee was all lined up with their guns ready, looking out onto the street.

"What's happening out there?" Bonnie said.

"Ain't nothing happening just now," I said.

"What do you think is going to happen?"

"I think that ole Chugwater's boys just might be a-planning another attack on us," I tole her.

"Will we be ready for them?"

"Look out there and tell me what you think," I said.

She actual got up and walked out into the office. When she come back in, she were a-pulling out her little Merwin Hulbert. "Everybody looks ready," she said, "but I'm going out there to help."

"That's good," I said. "Just keep yourself hid back behind the wall. Don't go sticking anything out where they can shoot it."

"Don't you worry about that none," she said, and she left me alone in the cell. I picked up my bottle and had me a good slug a' whiskey. I was

using my left hand to lift the bottle on account a'
if I done it with my right hand, it hurt my neck. It
come to me just then that I had might just as well
set in the cell and get drunk. I couldn't do no
shooting, the shape I was in.

"I'm going up on the roof with Happy," I heared
Butcher say, and right after, Churkee said, "I'll go
with you." I heared them run across the office,
and then I heared the back door slam shut. I could
also hear them climbing the ladder and walking
on the roof. I thought that was not a bad idee ole
Butcher had. Now they was three men on the roof.
They would get better shots at anyone down in
the street than what they could get from the front
winders. I tuck a good long drink.

"What are they waiting for?" said Polly. I was
a-thinking the same damn thing. To tell the truth,
I was getting kinda anxious to hear some gun-
fire. I didn't want no one shooting ole Chugwater,
though, on account a' I was really wanting that
privilege for my own self. And I weren't ready for
it. Not the shape I was in. Just outta curiosity, I
stood up and I hauled out my Merwin Hulbert
with my right hand and raised it up to the firing position. Goddamn but it hurt my neck. I
put it back into the holster and set back down.
I tuck another drink, and I seen that my bottle
was a-getting kinda low. "Shit," I said.

"They're coming out," I heared Bonnie say.
"Polly, can you pick one off with that rifle?"

"Sure I can, but I ain't sure I oughta."

"Barjack said to shoot them on sight," Bonnie

answered, and then I heared a loud report. It were a rifle shot.

"You got him," said Bonnie. "I think you kilt him."

I could hear Polly crank another slug into the chamber a' her rifle, and then she said, "I can get another one."

"Go on," said Bonnie. Then there was another shot and another cheer.

"That's two more down," Polly said. Then I could hear more rifle shots coming from up above me. Happy and Butcher and Churkee was a-shooting at the bastards from up on the roof. Pretty soon, the shots stopped. Bonnie come a-flouncing back into the cell.

"We run them outta town," she said. "Polly shot two of them down while they was mounting up, and then the boys on the roof started shooting. They dropped two more, and the other four lit outta town.

"That's good," I said. "And there ain't no more of them in town right now?"

"Not that we can tell."

"Well, I damn sure hope it's clear," I said, "on account a' I need someone to run over to the Hooch House and get me another bottle a' whiskey."

"I'll do it," she said. "I won't be long."

She holstered her little gun in that holster what was hanging around her neck and went out. Just as she opened the front door, she tole Polly and the others where the hell she was a-going. Knowing that I had another bottle a-coming, I lifted the one I was holding and drained it down. Then I tossed the bottle on the floor. Bonnie was as good as her word. She come back right quick with two more bottles. "I wanted to make sure you don't run out," she said.

"You're a right champion," I said, and I tuck one a' the bottles and popped it open. I tuck me a quick slug a' the good stuff, and it come to me that a slug out of a bottle what's just been opened is about the best drink a man can get. God, it was good. Bonnie tuck the other bottle out to my desk to put it in the drawer. When she come back she brung me one a' my tumblers. I poured it full. I meant to get my ass wiped out that night.

Chapter Eleven

Hell, I was just about drunken whenever ole Butcher come a-running in to tell me something. He was in such a hurry that he never looked where he was a-going. That empty bottle what I had throwed on the floor was a-laying right smack in his path on its side, and, by God, he stepped right on it, and it went to rolling, and it throwed him right down on his back on that hard floor. Well, he roared like a old bear, and when he hit, it sounded like a huge sack a' flour had been dropped from a second-story down onto the floor.

"My God, Butcher," said Bonnie, "are you all right?"

He never even answered her. He just moaned real loud. I set up on the edge a' the cot. "Get up, Butcher," I said. "Hell, you're all right."

"Oohh," he moaned. "No. No, I ain't. I can't even move."

I knowed that I couldn't get up (I was too drunk) and I couldn't help him up if I did get up (my neck was still a-hurting too much), so I just yelled out. "Help. Someone get in here and give us a hand." Bonnie jumped up and picked up that bottle and tuck it away to put it in the trash can. Churkee was the first one in, and then the rest follered. Churkee and Dingle got Butcher up onto his feet, but then they had to keep on a-holding him up. He couldn't keep hisself standing.

"Oh, God, I'm hurt, Barjack," Butcher said.

"Why the hell don't you watch where you're a-stepping?" I said, not showing no sympathy a'tall.

"Barjack," said Bonnie, who had come back in by that time, "that ain't no way to talk. Butcher's hurt. And how come you to throw your damned empty bottle on the floor thattaway anyhow?"

"I never thunk no one would go to stomping on the damn thing," I said. "Get him to a chair."

Ole Sly brung a chair to Butcher, and they eased him down on it. He groaned the whole way. "I'd better go fetch Doc," Sly said, and he left. When he come back just a few minutes later, he said, "Doc's coming. Barjack, Chugwater's coming too. I saw him ride in."

"How many men has he got with him?" I ast.

"He's alone," said Sly.

"That's what I come to tell you," said Butcher, kinda through his gritted teeth. "I seen him from on top a' the roof."

"He can't be up to anything too dangerous," said Churkee, "coming in by himself."

"That's what I figured," said Sly. "But he's coming."

"Polly," said Bonnie, "shoot the son of a bitch."

Polly went and grabbed up her rifle and went to one a' the front winders. "I can get him," she said.

"Don't do it," I said. "Leave him come on, and let's find out what the hell he wants."

"Barjack," Bonnie snapped at me, "we could end this all right now."

"I want to talk to him," I said. "Bonnie, fetch me out another glass." She went and brung me one. In another minute there was a-banging on the door.

"Barjack," a voice called out. "It's Chugwater. I want to talk to you."

"Let him in," I said, "but keep your eye on him."

Polly went and opened the door, and Chugwater stepped in. He stopped and looked around at the mess a' people in my office. He looked a little bit suspicious or maybe it was nervous. "Come on in here," I called out, and Polly pointed him to the cell where I was a-setting. Chugwater stepped in kinda cautiouslike.

"I don't like coming into a jail cell," he said.

"You said you wanted to talk to me," I said. "Well, that's where I'm at."

"I wouldn't stay in here otherwise," he said.

I poured him a glass full a' my good whiskey and offered it to him. He tuck it and tuck a drink. "Thank you," he said. "That's good whiskey."

"It's my own personal stuff," I said, "but I don't think you come here just to have a drink with me."

"You're right."

"Well, what is it?"

"How's my brother?"

"He's alive and being fed."

"That's good to know. There's been a lot of shooting around here."

"That there's your doing," I said, "not mine."

"Barjack, I can't just leave my brother in here to go to trial and maybe hang. I made a promise to my mother."

"And I think that there's a admirable trait what you got, Chugwater. I thunk a lot about that, and I don't know if I would be able to do the same thing for one a' my brothers. It shows you got a lot a' character about you."

"Thanks, Barjack."

"But I got my character and my reputation to think about too. I'm a lawman, and I seen Owl Shit murder that man to death. He done it right in front a' my own eyes and right in my own establishment, the Hooch House. I got to hold him for the judge, Chugwater. You had ought to be able to see that."

"I can see it, Barjack," he said. "And I admire you for your courage and your determination. You're a hell of a damn good lawman. I give you that. But there's men getting killed."

"All on your side," I said, "and you could put a stop to it if you was a mind to."

Just then there was a knock on the door. Polly hollered out, "Who is it?"

The doc answered, and she let him in. She showed him over to where Butcher was a-setting and still a-moaning, and Doc went to asking questions and poking around on ole Butcher.

"I see that a couple of you are hurt, though," Chugwater said. "I could call this thing off right now."

"All right," I said. "You do that."

"I said I could, if you was to release my brother to me."

"I ain't a-going to do that."

"I'd see to it that he showed up for the trial," Chugwater said. "Hell, I can buy off a jury."

"And Owl Shit could refuse to come to town for the trial," I said. "No, sir. That ain't going to happen."

"Then let's just you and me go outside and fight it out. Just the two of us. No one else would get hurt."

"I'd be just tickled to oblige you, Chugwater," I said, "but like you noticed, I been hurt. One a' your skunks shot me in the neck, and I can't hardly manage nothing with my right arm."

"That's too bad," Chugwater said.

"I'll damn sure let you know, though, when I'm fit to fight again."

"I'll be looking forward to it." He tuck a long drink a' the whiskey I had give him. "But I should warn you, that if it don't come pretty fast, I'll be bringing my entire crew in here to attack you. I mean to have my brother out."

"Or to die a-trying?"

"Can I talk to him?"

"Go right on ahead. Help yourself."

He drained his glass and set it down on the floor. Then he stood up and walked outta the cell. I leant back and pushed the blanket what was behint me to one side so I could see Owl Shit and Chugwater in the next cell. Well, Chugwater weren't in it. He were on the outside, but I could see the both a' them. When Chugwater stepped up to the cell, Owl Shit jumped up and run over to meet him.

"You come to get me outta here?" Owl Shit said.

"Not just yet," said Chugwater. "You got to have a little more patience. Barjack and his gang have damn near wiped out my cowhands. I had to hire me some new ones."

"Well, just kill the son of a bitch."

"That ain't near as easy as it sounds. Listen to me. I'm going to bring in the whole outfit, and we're going to fight it out to the finish. You just sit here and be quiet, and everything will work out for the best. You know I promised Mama, and I always keep my word, especially to Mama."

"I'll do my best. I'm sure glad you come by. They won't let me talk. I been quiet for the damnedest long time. It almost hurts to be quiet for so long. Say. Is there any way you can get me a drink?"

"I'll see."

Chugwater come back into the cell where I was a-setting. "Barjack," he said, "can I buy my brother a drink?"

I thunk about that for a short spell, and then I said, "Hell. Why not?" There was a little more than half left in the bottle I was a-hugging, and I handed it to him. He looked at me a little bit surprised.

"How much?" he ast me.

"No charge," I said.

"Thanks, Barjack," he said, and he walked back out. I leant back and pushed that blanket aside one more time to watch and listen. I seen Chugwater hand that bottle through the bars to Owl Shit. Owl Shit tuck it and tuck a fast drink out of it. He lowered the bottle and give his brother a look. Then he tuck another swaller.

"Thanks, brother," he said. "Bless you."

"Thank Barjack," Chugwater said. "He give it to me for you."

"Barjack did that?"

"That's right."

"But he won't let me talk."

"Try it. I gotta go now. You keep patient. I'll have you out of here soon."

Chugwater left then, and then I heared Owl Shit in a little weasly voice saying, "Barjack? Barjack?"

"What is it, Owl Shit?"

"Can I say something without getting no water throwed on me and without getting deprived a' my next meal?"

"Talk, Owl Shit," I said.

"I just want to say thank you for this here bottle. I sure was needing it real bad. I really do appreciate it. You ain't such a bad guy as I thought you was."

"That's all right, Owl Shit," I tole him. "That's enough talking now. You keep yourself quiet."

"Yes, sir," he said, and he shut up.

Butcher yowled out loud just then, and I figgered that Doc had poked him right where it hurt real bad. In another minute Doc come back into my cell. He come over to me and ripped the bandage off a' my neck and poked it a bit. Then he put on a fresh bandage.

"You'll be all right in another day or two," he said.

"Hell," I said, "I'm all right right now."

"Just you mind what I say."

"All right. Doc? How's Butcher?"

"Oh. Well, when he fell, he busted a couple of ribs back in the back. I taped him up real tight. That's all I can do for busted ribs. I gave him some laudanum for the pain. He won't be any good to you for a while now. If I were you, I'd send him home to bed."

"Well," I said, "the only thing is, you ain't me."

"Well," he said, picking up his bag, "call me again when another one of you gets shot or busted up."

He started out, and I said, "Doc, you send—"

But he interrupted me, saying, "I know. I can send my bill to Peester. He ain't paid the last one yet." Then he went out and shut the door behint him.

"Butcher," I called out.

"What, Barjack?"

"Doc says I should send you home to bed. You want to go home?"

"No, Barjack," he said. "I can't move around much, but I can still shoot if need be."

"That's what I thought," I said. "Good for you."

"Peester's coming," said Polly.

"Well," I said, "if he don't call out his name, kill him."

"Kill the mayor?" Polly said.

"That's our rule in case you forgot it," I answered.

Well, whenever Peester stepped up on the boardwalk, Polly went and shot his hat off his head. She didn't hardly have the nerve to shoot the mayor down like I had tole her to do. Peester yelled out. He bent over to get his hat, and he called out, "It's Peester. It's the mayor."

"Oh," said Polly. "Well, come on in, Mr. Mayor."

Peester come in holding his hat with both hands in front a' his chest. He was a-shaking something awful. Bonnie pointed to the cell I was in. Peester come in and seen me.

"Barjack," he said, "have you been shot?"

"No, I just daubed some ketchup on my neck and wrapped that there bandage over it for looks."

"I'm glad it wasn't fatal," he said, and I thunk for sure he was a-lying about that.

"What did you come over here for, Pettifogger?" I said.

"I want to know how you intend to resolve this situation."

"Which situation you referring to, Your Horniness?"

"This business with Chugwater and his brother."

"Oh, you mean with ole Owl Shit there in the next cell?"

"Yes. Chugwater's brother."

"Well, Your Orneriness, I don't know that there's anything to be resolved. Owl Shit kilt a man in front a' a whole bunch a' witnesses, including me, my own self, and I got him in jail. Ain't nothing else to be did. Is there?"

"Barjack, you know damn well what I mean. Chugwater's attacked this town already several times. He's going to tear the town up and get some more people killed. What do you intend to do about that?"

"I can't do nothing about it. I can't control Chugwater's brain, can I? If he keeps on a-coming on, we'll just keep on a-killing them."

"You could turn Owl, uh, his brother loose."

"Mr. Goddamn Mayorness, I can't hardly believe that I actual heared you, a bony fide pettifogging lawyer, say that. I'm a duly appointed officer a' the law. I can't just let a murdering skunk a-loose like that. The only way I could do that is if I had a order direct from you in writing and signed by your own hand and witnessed by three other citizens. It might ought to be signed in blood too. Your blood."

"You know I can't issue such an order."

"And you know I can't turn loose no killer."

Chapter Twelve

Well, nobody come around for a few more days, and I come to be kinda relaxed about the whole situation. I got damned tired a' being around the jailhouse with them same people all day and all night ever damn day and night, so I decided to get the hell outta there for a spell. I decided that I would go back down to the Hooch House with my Bonnie and hang around there. I might even spend a night back up in my room upstairs—with my sweet-ass Bonnie a' course. So I went and tole ole Happy that he was more or less in charge a' things while I was out, and I tuck Bonnie along with me and went on down to my saloon. We walked in there like we didn't have no cares in all the world, and we went back and tuck our usual seats at my private table. Ole Gooch Blossum were a-setting there in my own damn chair, and when he seen me a-coming, by God, he grabbed up his drink and scooted real damn fast clean acrost the room. I stood there by my chair and scowled at him for about a couple a' minutes before I set down. Bonnie was already a-setting.

Aubrey seen us come in, and he come over real

quicklike with our two drinks. "Anything else you want?" he ast us.

"No, Aubrey, that's all for right now, but keep 'em a-coming," I tole him. Then I went and tuck me a good long drink. Bonnie sipped at hers. It were one a' them pink things what she most always had. I kept a-staring at ole Gooch, and he seen me too. Final I reckon he couldn't take it no more. He got up and come all the way back over to my table. He stopped a few feet away from me; his drink was in his hand. I give him a mean, hard look.

"Barjack," he said, "Aubrey said you was staying at the jail. I wouldn'ta set in your chair if I'da knowed you was coming back in."

"Gooch, you silly-ass shit," I said, "you know that this here is my private table and this here what you set in is my private chair. Don't you?"

"Yes, sir, but—"

"And even if I ain't in here, they's still private and personal."

"Yes, sir."

"Don't you ever let me catch you a-setting here again."

"No, sir," he said. "I won't."

He backed off a few steps, and then he turned around and started to walk back to where he come from, but he stopped. Then he turned around and looked at me. He said, "Barjack, I don't see no harm in me nor anyone else a-setting in your chair whenever you ain't in here to use it."

"Oh," I said, "you getting tough now?"

"No, but I just don't see no sense in it."

I stood up, knocking my chair over back'ards, and I stepped right up to him. "Gooch," I said, "I mean to show you the sense of it."

I reached around behind his neck and grabbed a holt a' his collar, and then I shoved his head down till it was might near his own knees. With my other hand I reached out and grabbed his belt just above his ass, and then I went to walking him toward the front door. He was kinda like running all hunkered over like that, and whenever I reached them batwing doors, I reared back with him and then slung him headfirst through the doors. He sailed out over the boardwalk and landed in the dirt street on his face. He crawled a few feet on out into the street, and then he turned around to look up at me still a-standing there on the boardwalk.

"This is my place," I said, "and I make the rules for it."

"Barjack, damn you," Gooch said, "you went and made me spill my drink, and it weren't even half drank."

"Come on back in, then," I said, "and I'll buy you another one. I never said you was throwed out permanent."

He got up to his feet kinda hesitant, you know, but he follered me back in and back up to the bar. "Aubrey," I said, "get Gooch another drink. It's on me." I walked back to my chair and picked it up and set back down in it.

"You buying him a drink?" Bonnie said.

"I spilt his other one," I said.

I picked mine up and drank it down. Aubrey

seen me and come a-running with the bottle. He give me a refill. I don't rightly remember much a' what went on after that, except that I kept on a-drinking and getting refills. I think that Bonnie had herself a couple a' refills too. Anyhow, I reckon night come on, and I come to feeling just a little guilty. Hell, ole Sly and Churkee and Pistol Polly weren't even my reg'lar depitties, and I had left them down there in the jail while I set in the Hooch House a-drinking whiskey. Somehow, that didn't seem quite right.

"Bonnie," I said, "I mean to sleep with you up-stairs tonight, but before I settle in, I mean to go back down to my office and see is ever'thing all right. Do we still got a bottle up there?"

"I think you finished it off the last time we was up there," she said.

"Well, get one from ole Aubrey and take it on up there. I'll be right along before you hardly even know I'm gone."

"All right, Barjack," she said. "Hurry on along, then."

"Faster'n a goddamned snake," I said. I drained my glass and stood up. I was a little bit woozy, but I tried to hide it. Bonnie got up and headed for the bar while I kinda wobbled to the front door. I went out on the boardwalk and stood for a minute sucking in deep breaths of the night air to try and sober me up a little. Final, I turned and started walking toward the jail. I weren't moving too fast though, I can tell you.

I walked past one a' them little narrer spaces betwixt the buildings. It were real dark in there, and just as I got past it, two thugs come out behint me and grabbed my arms. Another one stepped out in front a' me and pulled a six-gun out and slugged me over the head with it. It hurt, but it only stunned me a little, and I groaned and said, "You goddamn sons a' bitches." He hit me again, and this time I went out. Ever'thing went black.

I woked up some time later, and I was a-laying on the floor inside a' some place, and my hands was tied behint my back and my legs was tied together. I struggled a little bit to kinda test the ropes, you know. They was tight. "Cut me a-loose from this," I said, "goddamn it, or I'll see you hang."

"You can't hang a man for tying up a dumb-ass town marshal," someone said. I twisted my head around to see who the hell it was. Up till then, I hadn't seen no one since the one that hit me over the head.

"You can't go calling a town marshal no bad names neither," I said. "I'll throw you in jail for that, and for assaulting a officer a' the law whenever you conked me over the head. You just don't know it, but I got all kinds a' shit on you, whoever the hell you are."

"Listen here, Barjack," the bastard said, "if I had my way, you wouldn't ever arrest anyone again. I'd kill you right now. Some of the men you killed was my pals. But Chugwater said no. He said we're to hold on to you and trade you for Owl Shit. Right now you owe your life to Chugwater."

"Oh yeah?" I said. "And what's your name, Chicken Shit?"

He reached out a foot and kicked me in the ass. "One more charge," I said.

"My name is Slim Carter," he said. "Remember it, dumb-ass marshal. I might get my chance yet to kill you."

"You might get the chance," I said, "but you won't live to enjoy it."

He kicked me again. "I'll live longer than you," he said.

"Slim," said someone else who was in the room, "cut it out. You know what Chugwater said."

"I ain't killing him yet," Slim said.

"Chugwater said don't hurt him none."

"Who went and busted his goddamn head?"

"I had to do that to capture him."

"That did more damage than a couple a' little kicks."

"Well, just cut it out now. Don't kick him no more."

"All right. All right. Hell."

"It tuck three a' you to get me," I said. "Where's the third one?"

"He's gone out to negotiate with your friends," said the second one.

"I don't reckon they'll trade for you," Slim said. "You ain't worth nothing."

"Fuck you, Skinny," I said.

"Goddamn you," Skinny roared. I reckon I really got to him final. He dropped down on one knee right beside a' my head, and he grabbed my hair in his left hand and pulled it hard, jerking my head up off the floor. With his right hand, he pulled out his six-gun and cocked it, and he shoved the barrel right against my nose. "I ought to blow your face off."

"You won't, though," I said, "on account a' ole Chugwater tole you to be nice. Didn't he, now?"

"You push me any farther," he said, "and I'll damn well forget what Chugwater said. His brother can hang and he can rot."

"Slim, damn it, I warned you," said the other one.

Ole Skinny's hand was a-shaking, he was so mad, but he turned a-loose a' me and my head fell back down and banged on the floor. He eased the hammer back down on his shooter and holstered it. Then he stood up. "Be quiet now," said the other one. Then I heared a voice come from out in the street.

"Hey, you in the jail."

It sounded to me like I was in a building just acrost the street from my marshaling office, and that third man I had ast about, well, he was out in the street a-calling out to them inside. I reckernized Happy's voice answering him. "What do you want?"

"Want to make a trade for Owl Shit."

"No deal."

"You ain't heard yet what I got to trade."

"Well, what is it?"

"We got your marshal Barjack tied up over here."

"I don't believe you."

"Open your door and look straight acrost the street. I'll hold him up in the doorway over here."

It got real quiet for a spell. "Don't worry. We won't shoot while you're a-looking."

Then the two inside jerked me up onto my feet and dragged me to the door. Slim opened the door and they pushed me into the doorway.

"Who's that look like to you?" said the man out in the street.

"Barjack," said Happy. "Barjack, are you okay?"

"I'm okay, Happy," I said. "Just shoot these bastards."

They jerked me back inside and slammed the door.

"Well, how about it, Deputy?" said the man in the street. "We got a trade?"

"Let me think it over," Happy said. "I got to talk to my partners in here."

"Well, talk it over, then, but don't be too damn long about it."

It got damned quiet then and stayed thattaway for a few minutes. Then I heared Happy call out again. "Come on out," he said. "Let's talk about how we're going to make this trade."

All three Chugwater cowhands went out in the street. They left the door standing open, and I could see out and acrost the street. Happy come out on the boardwalk, and Butcher and Sly come out too. It looked to me like as if they would have a fair fight if they was to commence shooting. And then they did. Sly gunned one a' them, Happy winged one and Butcher shot but missed. Then I seen ole Polly on the roof. She riz up with a rifle in her hands and snapped off two shots. One a' them dropped the man Butcher had missed, and the other one killed the one Happy had winged. I went to kicking around and yelling my head off. "Come over here and get me the hell a-loose from this."

Happy, Sly, and Butcher come a-running. Sly set me up. Butcher went to untying my hands and Happy tuck after the rope around my ankles. "Are you all right, Barjack?" Sly ast me.

"I ain't hurt 'cept where they busted me on top a' the head to catch me," I said. Happy final got my feet free, and I stood up. "Are they all dead?" I ast.

"They're dead," said Sly.

"Butcher," I said, "round up some boards and strap them bastards to 'em. Then lean 'em up against the buildings along the street here. I want Chugwater's assholes to see them when they come a-riding in here next."

"Yes, sir," he said, and he went running out. Me and Sly and Happy walked back acrost the street and into my office.

"Happy," I said, "run down to the undertaker's place and see if he's buried them others yet. If there's any that ain't buried yet, fix them up on slabs and stand them up out there too."

"Yes, sir," and he went running out and down the street.

"That's a good idea, Barjack," Sly said. "It'll put the fear in them."

"That's my intention," I said.

"How'd they get you anyway?" ast the Churkee.

"Aw, hell, I was a-walking back here from the Hooch House, and they jumped me from the dark space in betwixt two buildings."

"From now on," he said, "we ought to walk out in the middle of the street."

"He's right," said Sly.

"Yeah, well, we'll do that," I said.

It weren't long after that, Butcher had the first three bodies strapped on wide boards and propped up against the wall on the other side a' the street. I thunk ole Skinny looked particklarly stupid with his damn head a-drooping. Then here come Happy with another one, and he propped that one up a couple a' doors down from the first three. By and by, we had twelve bodies a-standing along the sides a' the street, all a-looking dead, which they was, and looking plumb stupid for it. I called Happy and Butcher back in.

"Good work, boys," I said. "That looks real good out there."

Then I seen Peester come a-running. I stepped out on the boardwalk to meet him. He was breathing hard and a-pointing at the corpses. "What's the meaning of this?" he demanded.

"That there is a message to ole Chugwater and his gang," I said.

"It's savage and inhuman," he said. "I want them taken down immediately."

"Yes, sir," I said, "just as immediate as Chugwater gets him a good look at them."

"Barjack, I'm the mayor, and I—"

"And I think you'd look real good standing out there with them," I said.

He shuck his head and walked away trembling. I started to say something more to him but decided against it. He weren't worth thinking too hard about. I stood there watching him go and admiring the work a' Butcher and Happy with their town decorations along the street. Final I went inside. First thing I done was I went to my desk and tuck out a whiskey bottle. I got a tumbler and poured me a drink. I tuck a good long swaller, and it sure did taste some good. Then I called the boys around and poured each one a' them a drink, but only Sly refused it. "Give it to Owl Shit," I said, and I seen Owl Shit jump up off a' his cot and hurry over to the bars, his eyes wide and anxious.

Chapter Thirteen

"Barjack!" said Butcher, who was standing at a front winder.

"What?" I said. I was a-setting behint my desk and sipping on a whiskey.

"Someone's just rode up outside. I think it's that Chugwater feller. Do you want me to kill him?"

"Is anyone with him?" I ast, getting up and starting to walk over beside him, carrying my glass with me.

"He looks to be alone."

Well, hell, ever'one else got to the winder before I did, so I just shoved them aside and stepped up beside Butcher. Sure enough, there was ole Chugwater a-setting on his big roan stallion and looking for all hell like the lord a' the manor. "I'll be damned," I said. Then I hollered out the winder.

"Chugwater, what the hell do you want here?"

"I come to talk to you, Barjack," he said.

"Climb down off a' your horse and hang your six-gun on the saddle horn," I said. "Then you can come in."

"You still got that jail full of folks?"

"Yes. I do."

"I want to talk to you alone."

"You got any a' your cowboys hid out around town?"

"Not a one. I'm here alone. I just want to talk, is all."

"All right. I'm a-coming out now."

"Barjack," said Butcher. "It might be a trick. Watch out for him."

"Aw, he won't try nothing on me," I said. "But go on ahead and lock this door after I go out."

I had my Merwin Hulbert strapped on around my waist and I was still a-carrying my drink. I walked outside and Chugwater come down off a' his horse. I stepped right up to him and tuck myself a drink.

"Can we go some place and sit down?" Chugwater said.

"Let's walk over to the Hooch House," I said, and so we done that. Neither one of us said a word whilst we was a-walking over. When we got inside, I seen that my private table was empty. I reckoned that the word was getting around about how I felt about that. I walked on back to it, and Chugwater follered me. We both set down, and Aubrey come a-running. Chugwater ordered him a drink, and I told Aubrey he might just as well bring me a fresh one. He hurried off, and in a minute he was back with two drinks. "Put 'em both on my tab," I said. Chugwater picked his up and tuck a sip.

"Thanks, Barjack," he said.

"What is it you's wanting to talk about?" I ast him.

"My brother," he said.

"You already know how I feel about that there issue," I said.

"And you know how I feel and how come," he said.

"Then it looks to me like we ain't got nothing to talk about."

"I want to offer you a deal," he said.

"What you got that I would want?"

"I've got twenty hands that will fight for me," he said. "I can send them in in a bunch, or I can call them off."

"Call them off and you'll save us both a hell of a lot a' trouble."

"I can't do that without you give me my brother."

"I ain't about to do that. You know that already."

"Barjack, think about what you're doing. You're holed up in that jailhouse pretty well, and if I come back in with my boys, you can kill a few more. We both know that. But with all the men I can get, I'll kill some of yours sooner or later. Might even kill you."

"You might."

"So if you give in, I'll call the whole thing off, and we'll save a number of lives. Ain't that what your job is all about?"

"My job is about holding up the law, and we got us a law against killing, especially unprovoked killing. Owl Shit done one a' them. I was a witness. I got to hold him for trial. Even you ought to be able to see that. Now, Owl Shit's got away with a whole hell of a lot in this town, and I'm sure in other places, on account a' whenever he gets his ass in trouble, you come along and get him out. But this time he's went too far. Not even you can help him."

"We'll see about that."

"Yes. We will."

"Barjack, I don't want to have to kill you."

"The way I see it, you don't have to."

"Without I get my brother out a' your jail, I do."

I drained my glass from the office, and then I said, "Well, you ain't a-getting him, so just put that thought outta your head."

"Barjack, you and me's been friends for a long time now."

"Well, we've knowed each other for a while," I said. "I wouldn't go no farther than that."

"You're a mean son of a bitch," he said.

"You ain't the first to say that neither," I told him. "Now, if you ain't got nothing better to say to me, I'll be getting back to my office. You can stay here and finish your drink, but I'm a-warning you. Don't bring no more a' your cowhands in here or else there'll be more killing, and you'll be the loser."

I stood up, taking my fresh drink what Aubrey had brung me.

"Barjack," Chugwater said, "no matter how many cowboys you kill, I can hire more."

"You got a endless supply a' money, do you?" I said. "We'll just see how fur it can go." I walked on outta the Hooch House a-leaving him setting there a-fuming. I headed back to my office, but on the way I got me a idee. I stopped by Peester's law office. I found the son of a bitch a-setting behind his ostentatious desk. He looked up, surprised.

"Barjack?" he said. "Have you settled your problem with Chugwater?"

"Not hardly," I said.

"Then what are you doing here? You should be at the jail."

"Mr. Mayor," I said, "can you put a hold on someone's bank account?"

"Put a hold? What do you mean?"

"I mean, being the mayor and all, can you stop a man from being able to get his money outta the bank?"

"I—I suppose I could, but who and why?"

"I want you to shut down ole Chugwater's bank account. He's got twenty men to be paying, and he says that if I kill all of them, he can hire twenty more. Just like that. We'll cripple the bastard if we stop him from getting his money."

"I see. Well, I don't know. That's a serious step to take."

"Do you think it's any more serious than killing more folks in our streets?"

"Well, no, but I—"

"Then do it, damn it. That'll come closer to stopping this trouble than anything else we can do."

"I don't know, Barjack."

"Listen, there'll be a election coming up again

here in a few more weeks. If the word was to get around how you went and stopped this wildness in our town, that would go a long way to making sure you'd be reelected, now, wouldn't it?"

He set and rubbed his chin some. Then he said, "Yes. I suppose it would." He stood up right quick and surprised the hell outta me. "Come on," he said.

"Where we going?"

"To the bank."

We walked on over there and went inside. Peester told the bank president to put a hold on Chugwater's money. We had to do some explaining, but final the old shit agreed to do it. Chugwater wouldn't get a damn dime outta the bank till we released his money. I actual shuck hands with Peester and said, "Thanks, Mr. Mayor. Now we'll get this thing settled, I'm sure."

"I certainly hope so, Barjack," he said, and I went back to the office.

Soon as I walked in the door, after hollering out my name to make sure no one tuck a shot at me, ever'one commenced to asking me questions all at the same damn time. I yelled out for them to shut up, and then I said, "One at a time. Go on ahead, Sly."

"What did Chugwater want to talk about?" Sly said.

So I went and tole them all about the conversation I'd had with ole Chugwater, including his claim to all the money in the world and how he could keep on a-hiring gunfighters to kill us all if

I kept on refusing to turn a-loose ole Owl Shit.
Well, that news give 'em all long faces. Then
Butcher said, "I seen you through the window.
I seen you go into Peester's office."

"What was that all about, Barjack?" said Happy.

So then I said, "Well, now, that there's the good
news," and I went on and tole them what me and
the mayor had did.

"Well, then, that's the end of it," said Pistol
Polly. "Ain't it?"

"Not quite yet," I said. "It will sure as hell slow
him down whenever his boys wants to get paid
again, and it'll damn sure keep him from hiring
any new ones, I reckon."

"He'll have some who are loyal," said Sly.
"They'll stick with him no matter what."

"We'll just have to kill a few more of them off,"
I said. "He claims to still have twenty men with
him."

"As soon as he finds out that you've stopped
him from getting any more money out of the
bank," Sly said, "he'll most likely try one more
big push."

"That's what I figger," I said. "So we'll have to
be ready for them. And that reminds me, how
come you and Butcher is both inside?" I looked
at Happy whenever I said that.

"Oh, well, we thought that it's been pretty quiet
around here for a few days," said Happy.

I said, "Get your ass up on the goddamn roof."

"Yes, sir," he said, and he went for a rifle and
then headed out the back door.

"It was my fault, Marshal," said Butcher. "I think it was me was supposed to be up there."

Pistol Polly was a-standing at the winder, and of a sudden, she said, "There goes Chugwater riding out of town."

I went and looked, and I seen him ride on out. "All right," I said, "we best be keeping our eyes open now."

I finished off the drink what Aubrey had poured for me, and then I poured me another one outta my office bottle. I set down behint my desk to try to relax a bit while I still had the chance. Bonnie pulled over a chair and set down beside a' me. She give me a hug that like to've upset me and my chair, but it never. It were about two hours later, maybe more, whenever Churkee was at the winder. He said he seen a couple a' cowboys riding in. I got up and went to look. I seen them. They rid right over to the Hooch House and tied their critters up and went inside. I hoped they would get too drunk to be able to shoot straight. Then two more come riding in. They tied up their horses too, but they just went and stood on the boardwalk and staring down in our direction.

Another hour went by, and they was twenty cowboys a-lining the street. Well, counting the two inside the Hooch House, they was twenty of 'em. Nobody had saw ole Chugwater, though. I wondered who it was a-giving the orders out there. I ast ole Sly what he thunk about it.

"Someone has got to be in charge," he said. "Someone has to maintain some kind of control."

"Chugwater coulda done made his plans out at the ranch," I said. "Give them their orders and sent them on into town."

"If there are twenty men in town," Sly said, "then the ranch is not protected."

"You reckon we should ought to hit it?" I said.

"It would seem to be a good idea and an excellent chance," he said. "The only thing is, we can't leave this place unguarded."

"You reckon how many we could spare?"

"I think maybe two of us could do some damage out there and still leave this place well fortified."

"Who do you think should ought to ride out?"

"How about you and me, Barjack?" he said. "It'd be like old times."

"By God, I like it. Butcher, go out and relieve Happy. Tell him to get his ass down here."

"Yes, sir," and Butcher was out the back door in no time. In another couple a' minutes, Happy come back in.

"Happy," I said, "me and Sly's going out to do a little chore. While I'm gone, you're in charge here. Ever'one hear that? Happy's in charge."

"Barjack," said Bonnie, her voice kinda pleadinglike, "where are you going?"

"Never you mind about that, sweet ass," I said. "Me and Sly is going out to do something. We'll be just fine. And we'll be back in a couple or three hours, I reckon. Don't worry your pretty little butt about it. We can sure as hell take care of ourselves."

"Be careful, Barjack," she said. "Mr. Sly, take care of him for me."

"I promise, Miss Boodle," Sly said.

Me and Sly went to the gun rack and supplied ourselves with rifles and shotguns in addition to the sidearms what we carried, and we stuffed our jacket pockets with boxes of extry bullets and shotgun shells. Then we went out the back door and slipped on down to the livery stable, where we got our horses and had them saddled up. Sly give me a look.

"Are you ready, Barjack?" he said.

"You damn betcha," I said. "Let's ride."

We mounted up and we rid outta Asininity the back way so's none a' the cowboys would see us. I was a-hoping that the damn cowboys wouldn't start nothing while we was gone, but if they did, Happy could handle things. I was pretty sure about that. Well, they never started nothing for as long as we was still within hearing a' the town, on account a' I never heared no gunshots. None a'tall. Neither did ole Sly. It was coming on night-time, and the sky was a-getting dark. We rid along easy, not wanting to wear our horses down none.

"What do you reckon we'll do whenever we get there?" I ast Sly.

"I figure we'll look over the lay of the land and decide then," he said.

I couldn't think a' no better answer, so I just let it go at that. We went along quietlike for the next several miles. Final we reached the ranch, and we rid up close to the big ranch house. There was a

light in one a' the winders. We didn't see no cowboys around.

"What do you think, Barjack?" Sly said.

"I think ole Chugwater's home alone."

"I think you're right," he said. "Let's burn his
barn for starts."

Chapter Fourteen

Well, we studied on the lay a' the land for a little longer, and we never seen no one hanging around. They was a few horses in the corral but not too many. We figgered old Chugwater had all a' his boys either in town a-watching the jailhouse or else out on the roads watching to keep ever'one in town and no one else from coming in. It sure as hell looked to us like as if he was at home alone. So we decided to move on out. We hauled out our sidearms just in case and we sneaked our ass down close to the barn. We opened up the door just a little bit so we could sneak ourselves in and look around. We wanted to make sure there weren't no horses or other critters inside on account a' we didn't want to hurt no animals. There wasn't nothing alive in there 'cept maybe some rats or such.

So we moved over to where there was a big stack a' hay, and we struck a couple a' matches and lit it on fire. Then we stood there and watched for a spell to make sure it was a-going good, and then we went back out the way we had come in. Looking around real careful in case someone should show up and spot us out there, we went a-hurrying back to our hidey place in that batch a' trees. We hung around there and watched till we seen the flames a-licking at one a' the walls a' the barn. Then ole Sly, he give me a look.

"Do you suppose we've done enough damage here tonight?" he ast me.

I had me a thought of a sudden, and I reached into my inside coat pocket and hauled out one a' them sticks a' dynamite I had been toting around on me. I helt it out for Sly to get a good look at.

"What do you reckon we could do with this?" I said.

He grinned. "We could sure shake him up a bit," he said. "Do you have a cigar in your pocket?"

"I sure do."

"Light it up," he said.

I tuck one out and poked it in my mouth. Then I dug around for another match and lit up. I puffed awhile and got it going real good. "Now what?" I said.

"Come with me." He led the way outta the trees and we walked a few feet closter up to the house. The barn was a-burning pretty damn good by then, but no one had poked his head outta the house yet. "How's your throwing arm?" he ast me.

"Well, it ain't what it used to be," I said.

"Let me have that stick," he said, and I give it to him. He helt it up with the fuse a-poking straight up, and he said, "Light it." I stuck the burning end a' my cigar to the end a' that fuse till of a sudden it went to fizzing and sparking. Sly tuck a couple a' steps toward the house and give a hell of a swing. It looked like a Fourth a' July celebration with that sparking fuse a-trailing through the air in a great big arc, and when it come down it lit right close to the front porch a' the main ranch house, where we figgered ole Chugwater was holed up all by his lonesome.

Then it blowed. The noise was deafening. It had been so damn quiet out there till that, that it damn near scared me half to death. It roared like a hundred thousand lions all at once. And the ground shook underneath our feet. A monstrous huge cloud a' dirt and rocks went up from where the stick had blowed, and a bunch of it come showering down on our heads. We couldn't even see the house no more for the dense cloud a' smoke and dust and other debris. Then there was the stench. It smelled like what a battlefield musta smelt like. All that burning black powder and such a-filling the air and our nostrils. It burnt my nose to just breathe.

The air cleared some, and I had pulled out my Merwin Hulbert, just in case. I noticed that ole Sly, standing to my left, had his Colt out too. Then we seen the front door a' the house come open and ole Chugwater stepped out onto his porch. He was a-holding a Winchester rifle in his hands and looking all around real wildlike.

"Who is it? Who's out there?" he called out.

We never answered him. Instead, ole Sly, he said to me, "Let's clear out." And we went to running back to where we had left our mounts. They was stamping around kinda nervouslike, I figgered from the noise a' the explosion. Sly was in his saddle first, and I was still a-struggling to get my foot in the stirrup. Sly rode up close beside a' me and reached down with his right hand, grabbing a handful a' my coat in the back and hauling me up. I swung my leg over and set in the saddle. "Come on," I said, and we lit outta there lickety-split as fast as ever we could make them nags move.

I reckon ole Chugwater heared the hoofs a-pounding on account a' he fired off a few rounds in our general direction. They was just wasted shots, though. I knowed that he couldn't see us where we was at. We was back on the road into Asininity in a hurry, but we knowed that Chugwater's boys was a-watching that road, so whenever we got close in, we swung around wide and rid through the prairie to come into town the back way. We come in behint the jailhouse and tied our horses there. Then we walked up to the back door and I pounded on it. "It's Barjack and Sly," I hollered. "Let us in."

My Bonnie ripped open the door and we went on in. Bonnie shut the door and bolted it back. When we went into the main room, ever'one kinda gathered up around us. I seen them all 'cept for ole Butcher. "Is Butcher on the roof?" I ast.

"Yes, sir, Barjack," said Happy.

"What's been going on in here?" I said.

"Nothing, Barjack," said Happy.

"You mean as long as we been gone, them Chugwaters ain't done nothing?"

Happy scratched his head a little. "No, sir," he said. "They ain't done a damn thing the whole time you been gone."

I scratched my head. "We was gone for quite a spell," I said.

"Yes, sir, I know you was," said Happy. "But they ain't done nothing but take turns a-looking at us."

"There was a time I thought they was going to make a move," said Polly, "but it didn't turn out to be nothing."

"Well, what did they do?" I ast.

"I was watching out the front winder," she said, "and four of them come out with rifles in their hands. They walked a few steps thissaway, and then they stopped and just looked. Pretty soon, they turned around and walked back."

"And that was it?"

"That was it."

"They were just trying to make us nervous," said Sly, "which is basically what we were doing out at Chugwater's ranch."

"But 'cept we done it a little more daring than what they done," I added.

"What did you do, Barjack?" said Bonnie, and she were just a-frothing at the mouth.

"We just burned his barn down," I said. "That's all."

"Burned the whole damn barn down?" said Happy.

"The whole damn thing," I said.

"That wasn't quite all," said Sly. "We tossed a stick of dynamite at his house."

"When that thing blowed," I said, "Chugwater come a-running out his front door with his eyes as big as bulls' balls and rolling all around in his head, looking this way and that, and yelling for all he was worth."

"Well," said Churkee, who had been quiet up till then, "I'd say of the two exchanges, you got the better of him."

"Barjack?" said Happy.

"What is it?" I said.

"Why don't some of us go back out there and do some more damage? Like maybe burn his house down?"

"If we was to burn down ever'thing he's got out there and even kill all a' his cattle, he'd still have twenty drunk cowhands in town to wipe us out. I think we done all the damage we can do out there. Or at least, all we need to do."

"Well, what are we going to do now?"

"Wait for him to make the next move," I said, looking at Sly, and he nodded. "We just now pissed him off a whole damn bunch. He'll do something."

Nothing more happened that night, but it were right early the next morning when I heared someone a-hollering outside. I got my ass up and went to my desk to pour me out a glass a' hooch. Then I strapped on my Merwin Hulbert and went to the front winder to look out. There in the middle a' the damn street was ole Chugwater hisself on his big horse. He had six cowhands standing behind him in the street, each one holding a rifle. "Barjack, goddamn you," he was a-yelling. I opened the door a crack and peeked out.

"What the hell do you want, Chugwater?" I said.

"You sorry son of a bitch," he said, "you burned my barn last night."

"So what if I did? You been a-bringing this fight all here to my office. I just figgered I'd bring it back out to you for a change."

"But my barn. Did you have to burn my barn?"

"I reckon we coulda come a little closter to your house with that there dynamite," I said.

"Goddamn you."

"Did you come all the way into town just to set in the street and cuss me?" I ast him.

"No," he said. He were a little quieter by this time. "I thought we could have us a little talk. See if there ain't some way we could end all this before anyone else gets hurt—or killed maybe."

"What you got in mind, Chugwater?" I said.

"This ain't no way to talk, Barjack," he said. "Yelling back and forth across the street."

"You got another idee?"

"We could get a table at the Hooch House."

"And have me in there all alone surrounded by your twenty cowhands? Bullshit."

"I could leave Oscar here inside with your people," he said. "You and me could go on down to the Hooch House. No one would bother you. I give you my word on that."

I looked at Sly and he shrugged.

"Okay," I said, "send Oscar on up here."

"Go on, Oscar," Chugwater said over his shoulder, and the cowhand on the far right stepped forward.

"Tell him to leave his guns behind," I said. Chugwater told him, and Oscar shucked his weapons, giving them to another of the hands in the lineup out yonder. Then he come a-walking on up to the front door a' the jailhouse. I opened the door wide and stepped aside for him to come through. I give him a look as he walked by me. "Boys," I said, even though two a' my crew was gals, "look after him real good while I'm out." I holstered my Merwin Hulbert and walked on outside. I walked right beside a' Chugwater plumb over to the Hooch House.

We went inside and I tuck ole Chugwater back to my private table, where I found three a' his cowhands a-setting. "Tell them bastards to get up from my private table," I said to Chugwater.

"Move it, boys," he said, and they scattered. We set down and Aubrey come a-bringing our drinks. Of a sudden, there was about eight cowboys all a-standing around me with guns pointed at most ever' part a' my body and hammers cocked.

"Hold it," said Chugwater. "Get back to your drinks. We have a truce called."

They put away their weapons and went back to wherever they had come from around the barroom. I tuck a swig a' my drink. Chugwater tasted his.

"Barjack," he said, "this is crazy. It can't just go on and on like this indefinitely."

"No, it can't," I said. "What do you got to suggest?"

"Let Owl Shit go free," he said. "We'll call it off. No more shooting. No getting even. It'll just all be over with and done."

" 'Cept only you win. Right? You get your way, but what do I get?"

"You and your people get to stay alive," he said.

"I can't do that, Chugwater," I tole him. "And you know that. Now here's my offer. You take all a' these cowhands back to the ranch, and just forget about Owl Shit. You get to keep your house and your crew. No more shooting. No getting even."

"Damn it, Barjack," he said, "you know I can't do that. I'd lose my baby brother, and I'd lose the respect of all my crew. They could never believe anything I said again. They'd never trust me."

"I coulda tole you how this conversation was going to end up. So that's all they is to it. They's nothing left for it but for us to fight it out to the last man. And I can tell you, you ain't a-going to win this one."

"By God, I will," he said, and he slammed his fist down on the table.

"We'll see about that. We'll see who lives to tell the tale. I reckon it'll be the stuff a' Dingle's next book."

"Yeah. Barjack's last fight," he said. "The Burying of Barjack."

"Just put in Chugwater where you said Barjack," I told him, "and you'll likely be right close to the truth. So now if this conversation is over with and did, I'll be a-getting my ass back to the jailhouse."

"I'll kill you before you leave this room," he said, a-pulling out his pistol.

"And who'll ever be able to believe you again?"

I said. "You told these boys that we had us a truce. Is that any way to end a truce?"

He kept his gun a-pointed at me, but he said, "All right. Get on back down to the jail, then."

I stood up and looked down at him. "When I leave," I said, "I want you to move away from my private table, and I want you to keep your men away from it too."

He stood up then and follered me to the door. I went on outside and headed straight for the jailhouse and marshaling office. Chugwater walked along behint me. I seen nervous-looking Chugwater cowhands all along the way, but they seen their boss with a gun at my back, and they never went for theirs. Whenever I was about six steps away from the front door to the jailhouse, Chugwater said, "Hold it right there." I stopped, and it tuck ever'thing I had in me to keep from showing how scared I was.

"All right, Barjack," Chugwater said, "the truce is over right now, and we're going to start shooting at the count of three."

"Open up for Barjack," I shouted, and I run for all I was worth for that damn door. Just as I was about to ram my head into it, it come open, and I went to diving headlong through the doorway and into the office. As I dug my old face into the floor, bullets was a-spanging into the door and the floor all around me. I don't know how many bastards was out there a-shooting at me, but it sure as hell sounded like as if there was a small goddamn army out there. Whenever my feet cleared the space, someone slammed the door shut, and then they went to shooting back through the winders and whoever it was up on the roof was a-shooting too.

I pushed someone aside at the winder and stuck my Merwin Hulbert out and tuck me a shot at that damned Chugwater. Either my aim was high or I jerked the trigger too damn much on account a' I blowed the hat off a' the top a' his head. "Shit. Goddamn," I said. I went to take aim again, but he run acrost the street and hid hisself in a doorway. I sure did wish I had aimed a bit lower.

Well, now, ever'one was shooting outta some nook or cranny, so I reckoned as how they didn't need me a-shooting too. I walked back to my desk and around it to set down, and I seen that Oscar a-setting on the floor with his knees all pulled up a-hiding from all the flying lead. I grabbed his shirt collar and pulled him up onto his feet. "Come on, Oscar," I said. "Chugwater sent me home, so I reckon it's your time to go on back as well." I walked him over to the door. I opened it a crack, and I yelled out, "Chugwater. I'm a-coming out after you." Then I jerked the door full open and shoved Oscar out. He were shot plumb to pieces before any a' the shooters tuck notice a' who it was they was a-killing.

Chapter Fifteen

Chugwater called off his boys right after that, and he called out to see would we let them pick up what was left a' Oscar. I told them to come on ahead, and I told all a' my people to not bother them whilst they was a-doing it. I knowed that Oscar would commence to stinking before too much longer, and that he would commence to calling up flies around the front door. I sure didn't envy them none, the ones what ole Chugwater made to pick up the carcass on account a' it was sure enough a mess from all a' them bullets what had hit it.

"How many of them did we kill?" I ast.

"Nary a one that I could tell," said Happy. "Just that one that they theyselfs kilt."

"Well, hell," I said. "They's still nineteen of them out there. And Chugwater."

"That means that there's still twenty that we got to fight," said Happy.

"I'm glad you passed third-grade arithmetic, Happy," I said.

"We can still handle them," said Sly.

I was glad a' his confidence. He had fought in many a range war and such, and if he had confidence in our chance, it give me some. Some but not too much. I was thinking about them twenty men out there. But ole Sly, the great widdamaker, he was sure a good one to have on our side. I couldn't think a' no one else I would rather have with me in a fight, especial a big one like this here was. I was amazed that we hadn't had no one hurt or kilt yet, and I was afraid a' what might be yet to come of it. And then I got to thinking a' how much it pissed me off to have all a' them twenty bastards over in my own Hooch House a-drinking my booze, and I betted my own self that they wasn't even paying for it neither. I was losing a fortune on this deal.

Well, by God, I would make up for it. Whenever the fight was over and did with, and ole Chugwater was deader'n hell, I would attach all a' his cattle and move them over onto my own ranch. That thought made me feel some better, but 'cept he weren't dead yet, and he still had nineteen cowboys a-backing up his play. I poured myself a glass a' whiskey and had a long drink. Then I went and offered it around. Happy tuck one and so did Polly and Churkee. My sweet tits Bonnie had one too. But Sly abstained. Dingle never even answered me. He just set in the corner with his pad and pencil a-scribbling. Owl Shit stood at the bars a-drooling, but I just let him drool. I weren't feeling none too kindly toward none a' Chugwater's family just then.

Happy finished his drink and said it were about time for him to relieve Butcher up on the roof, and so he went out the back door, and in another minute Butcher come in. I give him a drink.

"Thanks, Barjack," he said. "Say. I didn't see any cowboys fall a while ago in that shoot-out. Did we get any of them?"

"No, we never," I said. "They got one a' their own, is all."

Then I got to feeling real drowsy all over, and so I put my feet up on the desk and leaned back to catch a nap. It come over me then that I was getting a little old for this kinda life. It didn't take too much anymore to make my muscles commence to hurting, and I had to get to sleep earlier in the evening. I couldn't eat quite as much as I was used to eating. There was only a few things what I could still do that I used to do, and some of them hurt me whenever I done them. It come to me that I could just drop dead any ole time, and I didn't like that thought. At least not till I had won this fight with Chugwater. I would hate to drop dead and have him get ole Owl Shit outta my jail and gloat about it over my grave. Hell, they would probably even put the word out that they had kilt me instead a' me just dropping over dead for no real reason. I decided then that I would have to stay alive for a while yet. There just wasn't no choice in the matter.

I wondered as I was a-dropping off to sleep if I would be a ghost after I was dead. And I thought that if I was, I would damn sure ha'nt

ole Chugwater and his baby brother, Owl Shit. If I
knowed for sure that was what would happen, I
wouldn't mind it so much. I dranked up the rest a'
my whiskey outta my glass, and then my head
dropped onto my chest, and I brung it back up
with a jerk. I was fixing to drop off to sleep no
matter what, so I just kinda eased my head down
and relaxed.

After a while I'd had enough, so I just stood up
outta my chair. I poured another tumbler full a'
whiskey and dranked it down in two or three big
gulps. Damn but it was good. Then I walked over
to the jail cell, and I was startled to see the door
standing wide open. Owl Shit were gone. I looked
around and none a' my people was in the office. I
was all by my own self. "Damn it," I cussed, and
stamped the floor. I tried to figger out what might
coulda happened. I couldn't come up with no
way Chugwater and his boys could get into the
office and take over from my gang while I was
asleep and not wake me up. The only other thing
was if one a' my bunch had made a deal with
Chugwater, and they had broke up and let Owl
Shit out real quietlike while I was snoozing. But
who woulda done me thattaway? Who? Not Sly. I
couldn't imagine him a-doing me like that.
Happy? Happy were too stupid to make any deci-
sion on his own.

I decided that I weren't going to let this happen
without a fight. I checked my Merwin Hulbert,
and then I went outside and mounted up on my
ole horse. I turned him and rid outta town, going

toward Chugwater's ranch. It didn't seem like it tuck me no time to get there, and whenever I rid up to the house, I noticed that the barn were rebuilt. Damn, I thunk, he done a real fast job a' that, all right. Then as I got closter to the house, the front door opened and Chugwater come out on the porch. Owl Shit follered him out. They was both armed with six-guns and rifles.

They both commenced to shooting at me, but they never hit me even once. Their bullets tore my jacket and ripped holes in my hat, but they never hit me. Final they stopped shooting. "I mean to kill you both," I yelled out, and I pulled out my trusty Merwin Hulbert and went to shooting. They run back in the house. In another minute I seen them both come a-riding around from behint the house on their horses, and they rid fast right by me before I had a chance to react. They was a-whooping and hollering and shooting their six-guns in the air, and they headed right for a low mesa what was back behint me.

One side a' the mesa was low and they could ride right up on top if they went thattaway. They did, but whenever they got up on top, I was already there, and I was a-laughing at them. "I said I mean to kill you," I told them again. Owl Shit throwed up his hands over his head. "No, Barjack," he screamed. "Don't shoot me." But I just cold-blooded aimed at his face, and I shot a bullet right betwixt his eyes. His damn head exploded. Just like as if I'd shot him with a stick a' dynamite instead of a bullet. It exploded, sending brains and blood out in a shower all over the place. Then I got down off a' my horse and started walking toward ole Chugwater. "You're next," I said.

"You killed my baby brother," he said, and he pulled out his Colt what he carried at his side. He fired at me six times, and ever' one a' the bullets hit me in the chest, but they just went right straight through me and never hurt me one bit. I glanced down, and there wasn't no blood on me neither. I kept on a-walking.

"Damn you, Barjack," he said.

I laughed. "Who's got the last laugh now?" I ast him. The last I seen of him was just his face, real close up, and real terrified. He had turned white, and his mouth was open wide like he was a-wanting to scream, like he was about to, and then the wheels a' my office chair rolled forward, and I went over backward and landed on the floor with a hard thump what woke me up.

"Barjack," shouted Bonnie. "Are you hurt?"

I was, but I never let on. "No, hell," I said, "I'm all right."

I admit to being a little embarrassed at falling over in my own office chair like that, but I never admitted it neither, and I never said nothing about my weird dream a' being a ghost and going after Chugwater and his escaped brother. I did look over at the cell to make sure Owl Shit was still locked up, and he was. Ever'one else who was supposed to be there was there. Happy was up on the roof.

Well, I poured myself another glass a' whiskey to try to shake that damn dream outta my head, and I dranked it down pretty damn fast too. I guess it worked on account a' I quit having them goddamn images come up in front a' my eyes. I got to admit, though, that it were great fun getting shot through like I done and not even being hurt. I kinda liked being a ghost. I got to wondering if that was the way it was really going to be whenever I did get my ass croaked. I sure as hell did hope so. In fact, I still do. I got to recalling something ole Dingle had said a while back whenever we thought we was dealing with a ghost before.

What he said was that a ghost could come down and make love to a woman right in her own bed, and he called a ghost what done that a incubus. I remembered that there word too, and I determined that if I was to become a ghost I would be that kind. I would be a damned incubus, and I'd visit my sweet-ass Bonnie regular-like. I wondered if I should ought to tell Bonnie about that so that she could be looking forward to it, the same as I was.

I was pouring myself another glass a' booze whenever ole Sly come over and perched his ass on the edge a' my desk. He looked right down at me like as if he had something on his mind.

"What is it, Sly?" I ast him.

"Oh, nothing much," he said. "I was just wondering what Chugwater might be thinking right about now. He's got to be scheming up something."

"I reckon we've pissed him off right royal," I said.

"I expect you're right about that. I'm trying to

think what I would be thinking if I were in his position."

"Were it me," I said, "I'd be a-thinking about letting my little brother hang. That's where my head would be at."

"I don't believe he's thinking that way," said Sly. "He's too loyal to his family. Made a promise to his mother, and he's always kept it. Even without that, I think he's gone way too far to back down now. It's a matter of pride with him now. He's got to win, or die trying."

"I vote for that there last option," I said. I was kinda proud a' that word. I was getting me quite a vocabalary from ole Dingle. I liked to use them words any chance I got to just kinda show off how smart I was.

"I agree with you," Sly said, "but I haven't figured out just how to accomplish it. I suppose one of us could call him out and suggest settling the issue one on one."

"We could try it," I said.

"You don't think he'd go for it?"

"No, sir, I don't. Why should he risk his own worthless hide when he's got nineteen cowhands to throw out in front to get kilt first?"

"You got a point there. I'd still like to know what he's thinking."

Polly hollered out just then, "Come another step and you're a dead man!"

"Who is it?" I said.

"I don't know the son of a bitch," she said, "but he tied his horse out front and he's walking right up to the door."

I walked over to stand beside her at the winder and look out, and by God, I seed ole Custer, the county sheriff.

"Don't shoot, Polly," I said, "that there's the sheriff." Then I yelled out the winder, "Dick, you ole son of a bitch, what the hell brings you around?" I went and opened the front door to let him in. He come in and he looked around real curious at all the folks in my office and all the guns. "Come on over here and set," I said, and I pulled a chair over to my desk for him. Then I went back around to my own chair and set my ass down in it. I poured whiskey in my glass and pulled out another glass and offered ole Custer a drink, what he accepted.

"I ain't heard nothing from you for a while," he said. "Thought I'd come over and see how things're going."

"Well, hell," I said, "you can see how it is. We got us a armed camp here on account a' ole Chugwater. He's got a army a' cowhands out in the streets a-laying siege to the jailhouse a-trying to make me turn his little brother a-loose."

"Have you had anyone hurt?"

"No, I ain't, but we've kilt maybe ten cowboys. Maybe more. I don't know for sure."

Ole Custer kinda looked around again, and his eyes lit on Owl Shit in the jail cell. He jerked a thumb toward him. "That the brother?" he ast me.

"That's him all right. They call him Owl Shit."

"Owl Shit?"

"That's right. I think his right name is Merwin, but he don't like getting called Merwin." Whenever I said that there name, I raised my voice way up to make sure that Owl Shit could hear me real plain. I seen him kinda grimace too. But he knowed better than to say anything. He knowed he'd get splashed with another bucket a' water or something. Just then Polly said that she seen Chugwater ride up to the Hooch House and go inside.

"Barjack," said Custer, "is there any chance that, uh, Owl Shit, ain't really guilty a' this killing that you say he done?"

"He done it right in front a' my eyes," I said. "I'm the mainest witness to the damned deed. There was others too. It was done right in my Hooch House, and there was a passel a' folks in there drinking whiskey and beer and such. Most of them seen it happen. But mainly I seen it."

"Could you post bail and let Chugwater take him home till the trial?"

"I reckon I could do that, but I don't believe Owl Shit would ever come in for the trial if I did. That'd be just the same thing as turning him a-loose, don't you see? If he was really worried about getting hanged up, he might even skip the country."

"Hmm." Custer rubbed his chin, what needed a shaving. I went and rubbed mine too and found out that it needed one too. "Has he been outta town since he done the shooting?" he went on.

"No, he ain't, and that means that I ain't overstepped my jurisprudence none. He done the killing in my Hooch House right down the street, and I arrested him and brung him right down here to the jailhouse."

"I'm trying to come up with a way out of this bad situation you're in, Barjack, but if you won't set bail, I can't think of a damn thing."

"It all happened in your county, Sheriff," I said. "You could take over. You could bring a big posse in here and just take over. Hell, you could even take Owl Shit with you back over to the county seat. Now, what'd be wrong in that?"

"I can't do it, Barjack. I got to leave him right here where you arrested him. I got no men I can depend on anyhow. I'm sorry. It looks like it's your problem. It's local, and that's all there is to it."

"Well, Dick, goddamn it, just what is your job? What the hell was you elected to do? Look at me over here in little Asininity where I'm just the town marshal. Look at how many depitties I got here. I got Happy and Butcher, my two regular depitties, and then I got ole Sly, and I got Miller the Churkee. I've even got two women in here with guns. Bonnie and Polly. And I got that scribbling feller Dingle. How many is that? Huh? That's about eight, ain't it?"

"That's seven, Barjack."

"Well, hell, all right, seven. I said about eight. Seven is about eight. If I can get seven over here, you'd ought to be able to do better over yonder in the county seat. Your job is keeping the peace and enforcing the law in the county. We're in the county here too. So why the hell don't you do something about it?"

"I'm busy enough keeping order in the county seat and in towns around the county that don't have their own local peace officers. Asininity has got you, so I don't have any business poking my nose in over here."

"Then what the hell did you come over here for?"

Chapter Sixteen

Well, ole Dirty Dick left outta the office after Bonnie and Happy lit into him a little. Sly never spoke to him, just give him a nod as he walked by. I went to the winder to watch him, and I seen that he rid on over to the Hooch House and tied up in front and went on inside. I wondered did he just want another drink or was he going in there to talk some with that goddamned Chugwater? I wouldn't put it past him, but I never did find out. I went back to my desk and poured me another drink. By and by Polly, still peeking out the winder, said, "There he goes."

"Ole Custer?" I said.

"Yeah. He's mounted up, and he's riding back outta town."

"The son of a bitch," I said.

I was thinking that I wisht I had gone on to the next stage a' flying. I had learnt to fly that time Bonnie had tossed me off a' the landing over the barroom a' the Hooch House. I had sailed out over ever'one and just hovered there for a minute or two before I fell down and crashed on a table, breaking its all four legs and my nose. It was worth it, though, on account a' I had learnt to fly. The next time I were up on a kinda ledge and there was a owl hoot down below on horseback. I launched my ass out into the air and come down right smack on top a' the bastard, knocking him off a' his horse and breaking his fool neck.

The only thing was, I hadn't never gone the next step and learnt how to launch my ass without being on something up high thattaway. I really did wish I had done that. If I had I would justa raised myself up from out on the boardwalk and flew over to Chugwater's ranch to spy on his ass and figger out what the hell he was up to.

I tried to think up some way to launch myself. I thunk about riding a horse real damn fast till I just kinda riz up outta the saddle, but I didn't really think that would work. Maybe I could get in a wagon bed and start it rolling down a real steep hill and see if I could get going from there. But I was afraid it would crash into a tree or something. Final I had to give up on the whole idee. Maybe my ass was just too damn heavy to fly thattaway.

"Barjack," said Bonnie, dragging me outta my reverie. (That there was another word I had learnt from ole Dingle.) "Barjack, I need to have me a bath. Do you want me to have one set up over here again like last time? Or should I just have it drawed over at our room?"

It come to me that I could use one too, and so could a number of our companions. "You going over to the Hooch House?" I ast her.

"Yeah. I'll have Aubrey set it up."

"Have him set it up over here again," I said. "And have him send along that there smelly soap."

"I'll do it," she said, and she give me a slobbery kiss right there in front a' ever'one, and then she went on out the front door with her Merwin Hulbert pistol a-hanging around her neck. I went to the winder to watch her walk away. I loved to watch her from behind like that. Her two humongous ass cheeks flopped and wallered around whenever she walked.

After a while when she never come back, I commenced to worrying a little, getting downright aggravated. I reckoned she had got into a conversation with someone in the Hooch House, and that pissed me off. Whyn't she come on back? I knowed it would take a spell for Aubrey to get the tub over and to get it filled with hot water, but there weren't no reason for ole Bonnie to hang around over there while he was getting it did. "Goddamn it," I said, and I poured me another glass a' booze.

It didn't never occur to me to worry that she mighta got herself in some kinda trouble. I always figgered ole Chugwater was some kind a' gentleman, not like his sleazy little brother. He wouldn't bother no woman. I still had a lot to learn. By and by, I heared Aubrey's voice outside.

"Barjack," he hollered out, "it's Aubrey. Don't no one shoot at me."

"Let him in," I said.

Polly opened the door and Aubrey come in. He looked some nervous too. He seen me behint my desk, and he walked over to stand in front of it. "Aubrey, what the hell are you doing here? Why ain't you a-drawing bathwater?"

"I am, Barjack," he said. "Miss Bonnie came in and told me to have a bath drawed and fetched over here to the jail, so I give the orders, and it's being done."

"So why ain't Bonnie come back?" I ast him.

"She started to leave the Hooch House," Aubrey said, "but ole Chugwater stepped in front of her with a shotgun in his hands. He took her pistol away from her, and when she went to cussing him, he threatened to shoot her. He finally got her quieted down and had a couple of his boys tie her up. Then to keep her quiet, he tied a rag around her mouth."

I jumped up from outta my seat. "That god-damned bastard," I shouted. "What was you a-doing all this time?"

"Two of them cowboys was holding guns on me," he said. "Then Chugwater come over to me, and he said, 'Aubrey, I want you to go over to the jail and tell Barjack that we have his woman down here. Tell him,' he said, 'that if he ever wants to see her alive again, he'd better trade my brother for her.'"

He shut up then and I waited but he never said no more. "Is that it?" I said final.

"Yes, sir," he said. "That was all of it."

"He wants to trade Bonnie for Owl Shit?"

"That's what he said."

I thunk real hard about that. It were a chance to get myself free again, but then I recalled that time

I had got rid a' Bonnie and married up with ole Lillian, and I found out that I missed Bonnie real bad and Lillian made me near crazy. So whenever ole Sly come to town and he and Lillian hit it off, I let her have a divorce and let Sly marry up with her, and I felt like it was the smartest thing I had ever did. "Aubrey," I said, "tell him I'll do it."

"Just a minute, Barjack," said Sly.

"What? I got to save Bonnie," I said.

"We'll save her," he said. "But let's set up the terms."

"What do you mean?"

"You know back on the backside of town there's two empty buildings sitting right across the creek from each other."

"Yeah," I said. "I know them. One's the old mill. It ain't been used for years. The other one's a hotel that ole Angus McFarlan was a-building, but he went and croaked before he finished it. They sit right across Chugwater Crick from each other. What about them?"

"Let's tell Chugwater to meet us there. He and his men can bring Bonnie to the hotel. We'll take Owl Shit to the mill. Then at the appointed time, we can start the two of them walking across the bridge at the same time. That way, no one gets cheated."

"Sounds good to me," I said. Then I turned back to Aubrey. "Did you get all that? Can you go and tell Chugwater just what Sly said?"

"Yes, sir," Aubrey said. "I can tell him all right."

"What you going to tell him?"

"He's to bring his men and Miss Bonnie to the

old hotel and you're going to have Owl Shit at the mill across the creek. You'll start them both at the same time walking across the bridge."

"That's right," I said. I looked at Sly. "Was there anything else?"

"Just the time," he said. "It's getting a little late. I'd say let's do it in the morning. Say ten."

"That sounds good," I said. "Tell him ten o'clock in the morning, Aubrey."

"Yes, sir," he said. "Is that all? Can I go now?"

"Hell, yes," I said. "Get going."

Aubrey most run outta the office and went hurrying back down the street to the Hooch House. I could imagine ole Bonnie getting mad as hell on account a' me leaving her with Chugwater and his boys all damn night till ten in the morning. They had for sure better be glad they had gagged her up. I went to pacing the floor and chewing on the inside a' my cheeks.

"Barjack," said Sly.

"What?"

"Do you have any more of that dynamite you were packing?"

I opened out my coat to show him the five sticks what was still there in my inside pocket. "Good," he said. "Be sure to bring them along."

"I'll sure do her," I said. Then I told Happy, "Go out and bring Butcher down. And come back in your own self. I don't reckon we'll need anyone on the roof tonight."

"Yes, sir," he said, and he run out the back. When he come back in with Butcher, I called them all around. I told Butcher what the plan was, and then I told them all, "I want you all to get your guns ready. Clean them up and make sure they're in good working order. Load them up full. Ever'one take along a rifle or a shotgun in addition to your sidearm. And pack some extry bullets in your pockets."

"Barjack?" said Happy.

"What?"

"Are we planning for a fight or a trade?"

"We're a planning a trade, but we mean to be ready for anything what might happen. You got that now?"

"Yes, sir," he said.

I poured me another glass a' whiskey while ever'one got busy with their guns. I had my Merwin Hulbert and a shotgun and five sticks a' dynamite in my pocket. Pretty soon we was all ready for action. What I had told Happy weren't quite true. We were planning a trade all right, but after that I meant to wipe out Chugwater's bunch once and for all. I was pissed off at Chugwater now. I didn't have no more use for him. I meant for the action in the morning to be the final big battle over at the Rio Chugwater. Never mind that it was just a crick.

"I sure do wish I could have a talk with Bonnie before morning," I said.

"Forget it, Barjack," said Sly.

"Hell, I've let Chugwater talk to Owl Shit twice," I said.

"He's just proved that he can't be trusted," said

Sly. "He's taken to fighting with women. He might say he'd let you talk to her, and then he might just capture you too."

"Yeah. That's right."

"Barjack," Sly said, "be sure you have cigars and matches in your pockets."

"I've got them," I said. That reminded me that I could sure use a smoke. I tuck out one cigar and a match and lit the cigar. It were kinda close in the office, and I had it pretty near filled up with cigar smoke in a right hurry. No one minded, though. Leastways, no one complained a'tall. I leaned back in my chair, but not too far back lest my wheels got to turning again, and puffed at my cigar and sipped at my whiskey. Sly give me a look, and I pulled open the other side a' my coat to show him that I was packing a few cigars. Then I pulled out a handful a' matches and showed him those. I put them back in my pocket.

I sure did feel like getting drunk, but then I knowed better. I had a real important job to do in the morning. I figgered this glass a' whiskey would be my last one for the day, and I meant to really enjoy it too.

"I wish my daddy and his gang was all here," said Butcher.

"Well, they ain't," I said.

"I wish they was."

To tell you the truth, I did too. Them Five Pointers in New York City was damn mean and tough. If I'd had them, I coulda fought off three times as many cowhands as what Chugwater had out there. "Butcher," I said.

"What?"

"They would be a damn big help, wouldn't they?"

"Yes, sir."

"Barjack," said Sly, "I ought to go home and see Lillian tonight."

"You think you can make it without them seeing you?"

"I can," he said. "Even if they should spot me, I don't think they'll want to fight tonight, since we have the swap arranged for the morning."

"You might could be right," I said. "Well, go on, and good luck to you."

"I'll be back in the morning by eight thirty," he said, and he went out the back door. Polly latched it up behint him. Then she went and got Churkee and tuck him by an arm and pulled him into the extry cell what still had the blankets hanging up. I figgered I knowed what they was up to back there. They was awful quiet, though. It made me to miss Bonnie something fierce, and I sure did want to see her and talk to her and make sure that she was all right.

Happy was a-packing his pockets with boxes a' bullets for his six-gun and shells for the shotgun he was planning on toting. Butcher done the same thing, but 'cept he was carrying along a Marlin rifle. I went and got me some bullets for my Merwin Hulbert and some shotgun shells, on account a' I meant to carry along a Greener too. I thunk that Polly and Churkee had done loaded up their pockets, but I weren't for sure.

By and by them two come back outta the cell.

Churkee were looking a bit sheepish and Polly, she looked like she was a-feeling just grand. They put my mind back on my sweet Bonnie, and I had to try to come up with something different to put my mind on, on account a' I felt like as if I kept thinking on Bonnie, I were like to start in to crying. I sure didn't want no one to see me do that.

I got to thinking about how I would kill ole Chugwater and his baby brother and all a' his cowboys in the morning. I were really looking forward to that there. I figgered that we would make the exchange and then me and my depitties would commence to shooting. I knowed that in a fair fight we could kill them all dead'r'n hell. Course I didn't know just how dead hell was, but that didn't make a shit. We could damn sure kill them. I knowed that. We had did it before without no trouble to other damned owl hoots. I knowed we could do it again.

There just wasn't no one to match up with ole Sly. He was about the best, and I thanked my lucky stars that I had him on my side. And then ole Miller the Churkee, he was about as good. I hadn't seen many could match him. But 'cept that Pistol Polly. She was a match for Churkee. That was for sure. Happy and Butcher wasn't bad neither. They could both be counted on in a fight. I had been backed up by them before. Dingle, he weren't nothing to brag about, but he was game for a scribbler. My Bonnie was out of it for now, so I didn't count on her. But then there was me. Up against all them that I just named, I guess I weren't much neither, but I had come through a good many scrapes and I was still a-kicking. I meant to sail through this one more big one and still have both feet a-going too. Hell, I meant to dance on the graves of all a' them Chugwater boys.

Butcher and Happy was huddled up in a corner a-talking. I reckoned they was a-talking about the coming fight. Churkee and Polly was snuggled in another corner. Sly had gone home, I reckoned to diddle Lillian. I hoped that was what he was a-doing. I figgered that Lillian might could be a-chewing his ass out real good on account a' him helping me out the way he was, but I knowed that he could stand up to it, and I knowed that he'd be back in the morning. I was actual starting in to looking forward to the morning fight.

Chapter Seventeen

Well, I were up pretty damn early in the morning, and I got my guns strapped on and in my hands. I were ready to go with my Merwin Hulbert six-gun and my loaded shotgun and my five sticks a' dynamite in my pocket. I checked and made sure I had my cigars and some matches in my pockets too. Then I got to pacing the floor. I were nervous, anxious for the big fight what was a-coming, but it were way too early for that. I wanted a cup a' coffee, but I didn't want to have to make it, so I poured myself a good glass a' brown whiskey outta the bottle in my desk drawer. I set down behint the desk to drink it.

I was thinking about my poor Bonnie all trussed up over there in the Hooch House and I was sure a-hoping that no one had seed fit to molest her none. Damn, but I was hot under the collar. I was just a-itching to take a bead on that goddamn Chugwater and blast his ass all the way plumb to hell. By and by ole Churkee come awake. He had to untangle hisself from pretty Polly without waking her up, but he managed to do it. He gethered up his weapons, and then he went to looking for some coffee. Whenever he figgered out that I hadn't done nothing about it, he went and built a pot and put it on the stove to cook. Final, he looked over at me and said, "Good morning, Barjack."

"Mornin', Churkee," I said. "You ready to do some killing this morning?"

"I reckon I will be pretty soon," he said.

Happy come awake then, and he went straight to the coffeepot and poured hisself out a cup. He lifted it up to take a slug, but he stopped. He studied it for a minute or so; then he said, "This coffee looks like warm piss."

"Well, you dumb ass," I said, "it ain't finished a-brewing yet. Pour it back in the pot and wait a decent time. That is, unless you like it like piss."

He poured it back. He gethered up his guns and come over to the desk. Churkee was already a-setting beside a' the desk, so Happy just perched his ass on the desktop. "Should we be a-waking ever'one up?" he said.

"What for?" I said.

"Well, so they can be getting ready for what's coming," he said.

"Happy," I said, "what damn time is it?"

He looked around till he seed the clock on the wall, and then he said, "It looks like it's about seven thirty."

"And when is our meeting with them owl hoots scheduled for?"

"Ten o'clock, I think."

"So why in the hell would we need to be a-waking ever'one up yet?"

"I reckon we could let them sleep awhile longer," he said.

"It sounds to me like you're just a-itching to get to shooting," I said, and I was proud a' him for that, but I never said so.

"Yeah," he said, "I guess I am just a bit anxious to get it going."

"Well, don't worry none about it," I tole him. "It'll come."

"Yeah. I guess it will."

Then all three of us got to watching the damn clock, like as if the watching of it might hurry it on along. By and by, Churkee went over to the coffeepot and found the coffee was ready. He poured out three cups and passed them around. I was damn sure glad to get it, and I reckoned that the others was too. I had most near finished up my whiskey, so I poured what little was left into my coffee to kinda spice it up. Happy tuck a slurp a' his, and he said, "Now, that's better."

I heared a rustling noise and glanced over to the cell. Owl Shit was a-rising up from his night's sleep. "Happy," I said, "whyn't you give ole Owl Shit a cup a' that java?"

"Okay, Barjack," he said, and he went and poured a cup and tuck it to the prisoner. Owl Shit never said nothing. He just tuck that cup and went to drinking his coffee. I ain't sure if he was just rude or if he was still afraid to talk unless I tole him to. Polly woked up about then, and she looked around to find her Churkee. Whenever she located his ass, she moved over to set on it. "You want some coffee, babe?" Churkee ast her, and she said yes and went after a cup.

While she was up, Churkee stood up and went to pacing. I guess he didn't feel like being set on just then. Polly tuck her cup and went to the front winder to look out. "I see about twenty horses tied up in front a' the Hooch House," she said. I got up and walked over to take a look.

"Looks like they're gethered up early," I said.

"You reckon they been there all night?" said Happy.

"Most likely," I said. "I can't think a' no reason for them to go back out to the ranch and then back in here so damn early."

"You suppose they're anxious to get dead?" said Butcher, and that was the first I had knowed he was awake.

"They might as well be anxious for it," I said, "on account a' it's coming."

"There's coffee, Butcher," said Churkee, and Butcher got up and staggered over to pour hisself a cup. Dingle got up and fetched hisself a cup, but he went right back to the corner he had been setting in and went to scribbling again.

I said, "Dingle, goddamn it, how can you make your brain go to working like that first thing in the morning?" He never answered me none, so I never said no more to him neither. I had finished up my coffee, so I poured myself another glass a' whiskey. Churkee seen me, and he reached for my empty cup. "You want some more, Barjack?" he said.

"No," I said, "one was a-plenty."

He went on over to the pot and poured hisself some more, and I guess we musta dranked up that whole damn pot. He set his cup aside and went to build another pot. I looked over at the clock and seed that it was about eight by then. I thunk, Time is sure a-creeping by. I wondered if my Bonnie was a-sleeping or what. I wondered what would happen to ole Chugwater if she wasn't awake on her own by ten. I hadn't waked her up in the morning before about ten since that morning I woked her up to tell her something and she got so mad she threw me off a' the landing and I had flowed. It made me chuckle to think about it.

Owl Shit was a-standing by the bars holding his empty cup and looking forlorn. I helt up my bottle and called out to him, "You want to wait for the coffee to make or would you ruther have a snort a' this here stuff?"

"I'd be happy with a snort a' that there," he said, and he was most nearly smiling. I pulled another glass outta my desk drawer and helt it out to Happy. I give him the bottle too.

"Pour a snort a' this out for Owl Shit," I said. "He might be dead before the day's over." He done it. Then he put the bottle down on my desktop and walked over to the cell, where he give that glass a' whiskey to Owl Shit.

"Here you go," he said.

Owl Shit tuck it like he didn't think he'd ever see another one, but he never drank it down too fast. He kinda sipped at it. I guess he wanted to make it last awhile, you know. I tuck out a cigar and lit it and puffed at it to get a-going. I checked to make sure I still had some more in my pocket as well as some more matches. I had a-plenty. I kicked back in my chair again to smoke and drink, but I was still careful to not lean back too far. In a while I looked back at the clock, and I seed that it were damn near nine. And sure enough, I heared Sly's voice at the back door. He called out his name to keep from getting shot at, and Polly went and opened the door for him. He come a-walking into the office, and he did look sharp. I think he'd had hisself a bath and a shave and had put on a clean suit a' clothes. He smiled and said, "Good morning, folks."

"Howdy, Sly," I said. "I been a-looking for you."

"I said I'd be here at nine o'clock," he told me.

"You made it with one minute to spare," I said. "What the hell's that basket you're a-hauling over your arm?"

"Hot biscuits from Lillian," he said.

Well, we all dug in, and they was even a tub a' butter in there. The second pot a' coffee had done boiled, so ever'one had a refill a' coffee to go with his biscuit.

"Barjack," said Polly, who was back at the winder again, "the Chugwaters is moving out."

Me and Sly hurried over to the winder to look out, and sure enough, they had all mounted up and was riding, not toward the jail, but in the opposite direction. They was a-heading for the old hotel. I seed Bonnie a-setting horseback up front and Chugwater were riding right alongside of her. "Goddamn him," I said.

We watched till they was outta sight.

"Do we go now, Barjack?" said Happy.

"We'll give it another half hour," I said. "We ain't s'posed to meet up with them till ten."

I had myself a second buttery biscuit and looked at the clock again. It was nigh onto nine thirty. I picked up my shotgun and walked to the back door. Looking back, I said, "Let's all go. Happy, bring out Owl Shit."

Happy went and got the prisoner out and walked him up to right beside a' me, and then I led the way outta the jailhouse. Oh, the fresh air smelt good. I had finished up my cigar some time back, so I tuck out a fresh one and lit it, giving Sly a look. He grinned back at me. Then I started out a-walking with all the rest falling in behint me.

"Keep a lookout for any dirty tricks along the way," I said, and I was looking at all the rooftops and in all a' the dark corners and doorways. We walked down the alley for a ways, but before we come to the end a' the street, I turned to my right and we crossed over to the next street. If we had a-gone to the end a' the street and then turned, they coulda seed us a-coming and tuck potshots at us before we could reach the mill. Final, we come out behind the mill where we could see it just ahead of us, and I stopped. "Ever'one gether around," I said.

They all come around me. "No one shoot," I said. "We got us a agreement. I'm going to call out to ole Chugwater, and we're a-going to start Owl Shit and Bonnie a-walking at the same time. Anyone takes a shot while that's going on will have to answer to me. Does ever'one understand that?"

"But once I'm across that bridge," said Owl Shit, "all bets are off. I told you that you couldn't hold me in that damn jail of yours. You'll be dead before suppertime."

I whopped him acrost the back a' his head with the stock a' the shotgun what I was a-toting, not hard enough to knock him out, but hard enough to hurt like hell. "Ow," he said, and he leaned forward and shuck his head some.

"You keep your goddamn mouth shut, Owl Shit," I said, "or the next time I'll knock you flat, and I mean it too." He straightened up, still a-shaking his head. "Now come on," I said, and I walked them all acrost the way till we went in the back door a' the old mill.

It were dark and dank and dingy in there. It smelled a' something stale. I walked us all plumb through to the front wall what was mostly all winders. They was mostly all broke and gone, but there was one winder what still had glass in it. I looked acrost Chugwater Crick, and I could see the old hotel. It looked pretty damn sorry too. It had a porch in front with a roof over it. I guess they had tied their horses out back on account a' I couldn't see no horses nowhere. Owl Shit headed for the front door, but I clicked back both hammers on my shotgun and poked the barrels right into his ugly face. He stopped still, and his face turned white.

"You move when I tell you to move," I said. "Now get over there to the other side a' the door."

"Yes, sir," he mouthed, but I didn't hardly hear him say nothing a'tall. I went to studying the hotel acrost the crick. I couldn't hardly tell nothing about it. I squinnied my eyes at the winders in front a' the place, but I still couldn't tell nothing. "Sly," I said, and he walked up beside me. "Do you reckon them bastards is in there? Or could they have gone off somewheres else?" He studied on it for a spell.

"It's hard to tell, Barjack," he said. "But where else could they have gone?"

"Damned if I know," I said. "Do you got a watch on?"

He pulled a gold timepiece outta his vest pocket and studied it. "I make it to be about ten minutes before ten," he said.

"Let's take our time, then," I said, and I puffed at my cigar. I went and lowered them hammers too on my shotgun. I didn't want to take no chances on shooting that damn thing off by accident.

"Barjack," said Sly. "They're in there all right. I just got a glimpse of a man in an upstairs window."

"Where?" I said, and I went to looking.

"He was in that window on the far right upstairs," Sly said. "I don't see him anymore, but he's there."

"By God," I said, "they're a-waiting for us. They ain't got no intentions a' trading with us and then going home. They mean to kill us all for sure." I didn't say nothing about the fact that them was our own very intentions. I didn't mean for Chugwater nor Owl Shit nor none a' them cowboys to ride outta Asininity alive.

"We're ready for them," said Sly.

"You goddamn right," I said.

Then I decided that we had waited long enough. I went and stepped out the front door and stood there for a minute a-showing myself, and then I hollered, "Chugwater. Hey, Chugwater, you over there?"

In another minute Chugwater stepped out on the porch. He had a man on each side of him. "I'm here, Barjack," he yelled.

"I've got Owl Shit," I called out. "You got Bonnie?"

"She's here, and she's unharmed."

"Bring her out," I said.

"Let me see my brother."

Over my shoulder I said, "Owl Shit, step out here."

He come out, and he acted like as if he was going to just start in a-walking.

"No, you don't," I said. "You stand right there."

He stopped right in front a' me.

"Where's Bonnie?" I called.

Chugwater said something to his boys what I couldn't hear, and in another minute they brung her out on the porch. I could tell from that distance that she were madder'n a goddamn hornet. I was a-hoping that her mad was all directed at Chugwater and none of it at me, but I couldn't worry none about that just then.

"Let's get them started," I yelled. Bonnie walked

forward to the steps and then started down. "Go on," I said to Owl Shit, "but walk slow or I'll empty this scattergun in your butt. He moved out real slowlike. Bonnie was down on the ground by then and walking slow toward the bridge. The two of them was moving at about the same pace. When Bonnie got closer to the bridge, I could see her face plainer, and I could see that she were real damn mad, but I could see too that she was afraid. I don't know just what I were hoping for, but I were sure a-hoping for something.

I got to watching Bonnie, the way she moved, and even under these here circumstances, she was something to watch, the way her big hips was a-swinging from side to side. I thought she was for sure a grand woman. They got a little closer and both of them stepped up on the bridge at the same time. They kept a-walking along real slow-like. I could hear the bridge a-creaking when they walked, and I was sure hoping that them old boards would hold up under that weight.

Chapter Eighteen

Bonnie and Owl Shit come alongside a' one another. Bonnie were still a-swinging her huge hips
while she walked. Owl Shit were walking real
slow and easy on account a' he believed, I'm sure,
that I'da shot him in the back if he was to start
hurrying along. Then of a sudden, Bonnie swung
her hips real hard to the side and caught Owl Shit
with a good hard whump, knocking his ass to the
side, and he crashed right through the handrail
what was on the side a' the bridge and went
a-splashing down into the crick below. He yelled
some furious as he fell. Bonnie had swung her
own ass so hard that she went right in after him
and landed on top a' him down in the water.

Well, ole Chugwater, when he seen that, raised
up his own rifle and tuck aim at me, but I dodged
his shot real neatlike and fired a blast a' my shotgun at him. He yelped and ducked back into the
hotel. All hell broke loose then. Gunshots was
a-coming outta the hotel winders and front door
and spanging into the mill all over. I ducked behint a post a' the overhanging roof there. They
was a shed down close to the crick, and I yelled at

Bonnie. "Bonnie, get your ass up to the shed, and bring Owl Shit with you."

I reckon Owl Shit didn't have no breath left in him after Bonnie had landed her lard ass on top of him, and she grabbed him by the collar and dragged him outta the water with her and then ran up to the shed. She fell down with him on the mill side a' the shed with bullets hitting in the dirt all around her. My God, but she was a wonder. I thunk about calling out to her again to bring Owl Shit on over to the mill with the rest of us, but I was a-feared that she would never make it with all them gunshots going on. I was a-feared to make a move my own self.

Out of a corner of my eye, I seen Polly make a rifle shot outta one a' the winders, and I looked back toward the hotel and seen one a' Chugwater's boys come a-crashing through a upstairs hotel winder and fall to the ground below. He didn't move after that, and I figgered that Polly had kilt him. So they was only eighteen left. I hollered back over my shoulder, "Boys, cover me." Ever'one inside the mill commenced firing most at once, and I turned and run back inside through the front door. They was so many bullets flying, I don't know how I made it inside without being hit, but I did. I pressed my ass against the wall just inside a' the door. Then I sneaked a peek out and looked over to where Bonnie and Owl Shit was huddled behint the shed.

Owl Shit musta been about to recover, on account a' I seen him struggling to set up. Bonnie wound up and slugged him right hard against his jaw, and he dropped again. He were out cold. I could tell. Even so, I didn't like seeing her stuck over there away from the rest of us. I looked around, gauging my men. The best bet seemed to be ole Churkee. "Churkee," I said, "do you think you can get your ass over there to Bonnie without getting it shot?"

He tuck a look. "I can make it," he said.

"We'll all cover you the best we can," I said. "When you get over there, watch for a chance to get Bonnie and Owl Shit back over here, but don't take no chances."

"Okay," he said. He got hisself against the wall just inside the doorway right opposite to where I was at. He watched for a bit, and then said, "Now?"

I said, "Ever'one go to shooting."

I couldn't see no one over there to shoot at, so I just shot into the winders. I think ever'one else was doing the same, but we had such a barrage a-going that it kept the Chugwater boys' heads down so that they weren't shooting back at us. Churkee bolted. He run low and in a wiggly line, but only a couple a' bullets hit the dirt somewhere near his feet while he was a-running. When he got close to the shed, he made a dive, and he rolled up right close to Bonnie where she was a-setting. I seen her give him a hug like as if she were sure glad to have him there. I thunk, though, that it was not much of a greeting for him to be bear-hugged like to death. But I was sure glad that Churkee was over there with her. Sly moved over beside a' me.

"What now, Barjack?" he said.

"We need to try to get them three back over here with us," I said. I puffed on my cigar like as if it were going outta style.

Sly give me a look. "Barjack," he said, "if we were to blow up a stick of dynamite right in front of the hotel, that should distract them for a minute while Miller gets Bonnie and Owl Shit back over here."

My eyes musta lit up at that suggestion. I don't know why in hell I hadn't thunk about it my own self. I opened out my jacket and pulled out a stick a' that stuff. I helt it out for Sly to look at. "You want me to throw it?" he said.

"I think you got the best arm," I said.

He tuck it in his right hand and helt it out for me. I puffed on my cigar and then tuck it and touched the lit end to the fuse on the dynamite. It caught of a sudden and went to spewing. Then he stepped outside and even a few steps out in front a' the mill, and the rest of us went to shooting to keep the heads acrost the way inside and give him a chance. Sly reared back and flung that dynamite about as hard as he could fling, I reckon. I watched it arc way up and over, a-slinging a trail a' fizz as it went on its way. Sly come a-diving back in through the open front door. He hit the floor and rolled, coming back up on his feet. That spewing stick landed just in front a' the porch a' the hotel, and in another couple a' seconds, it blowed.

Churkee figgered out what we was a-doing, and he grabbed Owl Shit and said something to Bonnie, and the three of them come a-running back to the mill. In the background, behint them, there was a shower a' dirt as big as anyone coulda wanted. No one in the hotel coulda saw nothing through that cloud. My ears was a-ringing from the sound a' the blast. Churkee hit the front a' the mill and shoved Bonnie in first; then he shoved Owl Shit through the door, and final he come through hisself. The smoke and dust cleared about then, and the Chugwaters went to shooting again. We was all of us a-huddled back outta sight, though, and the bullets wasn't doing us no harm.

I couldn't help myself. I grabbed Bonnie and give her a bear hug a' my own. I slobbered a kiss on her too. When she got over her astonishment at what I had did, she squeezed me back and like to stopped my breathing, and then she slobbered a great big kiss on me. Whenever I recovered, I stepped back so I could look her in the face, and I said, "Bonnie, my darling sweet tits, I was never so glad to see you before in my whole and entire life. You ain't hurt, is you?"

"Oh, Barjack," she said, "I'm all right. But I am sure as hell glad to be back with you."

"Bonnie, you done real good out there," I tole her, and I meant it. "It were a stroke of genius the way you knocked ole Owl Shit off a' that bridge. I'm so proud a' you I just don't know how to tell you."

"Barjack," she said, and she went and squoze me again.

The gun shooting had started up again by then,

so I broke loose and went back to the winder. I seen a couple a' bodies laying out on the ground. I don't know who done it, but someone on our side had got in a couple a' good shots. I figgered at best they was only sixteen a' the bastards left over yonder. I were looking for something to shoot at, when of a sudden about eight or ten a' the sons a' bitches come out the front door a' the hotel with their guns a-blazing. They had decided on a full frontal assault against us, and they was a-coming hard and fast. I didn't have much time to think about it. I just jerked another stick a' dynamite outta my pocket and lit it with my cigar, and then I stepped out and throwed it. I felt a couple a' bullets tear through my coat, but I never felt none of them tear through me.

"Look out," one a' the bastards yelled when he seen what I had did. Then they all stopped and turned and started to run off in different directions, but they wasn't fast enough. That dynamite landed in the big middle a' the shit-asses, and in another second it blowed. This time I watched the big cloud go up, and I seen it carry some bodies with it. I ain't sure how many of them it kilt, but there was at least five bodies laying around whenever the dust died down.

"Good shot, Barjack," said Sly.

"Aw, hell," I said, "they was a-coming at me, getting closer."

"Barjack, you dirty skunk," said Owl Shit, "you cheated."

"What the hell are you talking about?" I said.

"We had all agreed," he said. "This was supposed to be an exchange a' prisoners. You cheated whenever you went to shooting."

"Well, hell," I said, "the situation changed whenever you fell off a' the bridge."

"I never fell," he said. "I was pushed."

"You wasn't pushed," said Bonnie. "I knocked your ass off into the crick."

"It was still cheating," he said.

"Owl Shit," I said, "I'm just going to say one more thing about it and that's all. All bets was off whenever your snake-in-the-grass bastard brother went and tuck a woman, my sweet Bonnie, for a hostage. Any man what would make war on a woman ain't deserving a' no considerations. And I don't want to hear you say nothing more about it neither. That was the last word."

He opened his mouth like as if he wanted to say something more, but he thunk better of it and kept quiet. I pointed to an old box setting over against the wall. "Now set down there and keep your yap shut," I said, and he did.

I went back to the winder looking for a target. Happy and Butcher was both a-sniping at something over there. Dingle was setting way back outta the way a-scribbling. Bonnie was right beside a' me looking out the winder. I could tell she were just a-itching to get into the action.

"Did anyone bring me a gun?" she said.

I looked back at Dingle. "He ain't using his," I told her. "Take it."

Bonnie went back and snatched the rifle what Dingle had brung along. He glanced at her as she done it, but he never said nothing. I reckon he was about as busy as he could stand it already. Bonnie come back beside a' me and looked out the winder. Just as she did, a Chugwater puncher stepped out on the porch with a rifle and tuck aim at us. Bonnie shouldered her rifle right quick and snapped off a shot and dropped that son of a bitch right away. I hugged her and kissed her fat cheek, and she grinned real big.

The shooting from across the crick slowed down and like to stopped. I don't know how come. Could be they was getting picked off too easy and needed a break. Anyhow, I was getting kinda tired of it all my own self. I asked ole Sly, "How'd you like to toss another stick a' dynamite?"

"Just fine," he said, so I pulled out another one and give it to him. Then I puffed on my cigar again and lit the fuse. "I'll get it closer this time," he said, and he stepped outside. A couple a' bullets hit near him as he stepped on out farther, and then he hove it with all a' his might, and he turned and come a-running back in. It flowed high and real purty this time. I liked watching it sail through the air and a-knowing what would come whenever it hit. This one was a grand throw. It landed on the roof over the porch, and when it blowed, sticks and splinters went ever'where.

It was a truly wonderful blast, a cloud a' smoke and dust and wood, and when it went to clearing some, we could see that the porch roof was plumb gone and part a' the front wall a' the building was gone too. What was left was on fire. Several cowhands had come a-staggering and coughing through the cloud a-holding their hands up over their heads. I looked for Chugwater, but I couldn't find him. I stepped out in front a' the mill with my Merwin Hulbert in my hand, and ole Sly, he stepped out beside a' me. I reckon that Owl Shit, he couldn't stand the tension, so he jumped up from where he was a-setting and come running out to stand beside us and see what was going on.

"Are you boys a-giving it up?" I yelled out.

"We quit, Marshal," one of them yelled. "We don't want to get blowed to bits."

"Throw your guns down in the dirt," I said, "and come a-walking slow over that bridge."

They all done what I tole them to do. They throwed their guns down and walked to the bridge and come a-walking over it. I called out to Happy and Butcher, "Keep these boys all covered. March them around to the back a' the mill and hold them there."

"Let's go," Happy said, and they started in to walk, but I stopped them.

"Hold it a minute," I said. "Is they any more a' you over there in that hotel?"

"No one but the boss," said one a' the cowhands.

"Are you sure a' that?" I ast him. "If I find out there's any more a' you cowboys still over there, it'll go hard on you."

"No," he said. "There ain't no more. Just only Chugwater. He wouldn't quit. He called us chickenshits and told us to go on ahead. He said he didn't need us nohow."

"Okay," I said. "Take them on away."

Happy and Butcher marched them on outta sight. I turned to Sly. "What do you reckon we'd ought to do now?" I said.

"We could march on over there and go looking through the building. What's left of it."

"We could," I said.

"I wouldn't recommend it, though."

"No?"

"Nope. He could be lurking in one of those rooms and waiting to drop us from ambush."

"Yeah."

"How much dynamite you have left?"

"Couple a' sticks," I said.

"Let's toss them and see what develops."

I drawed one of them out and give it to him. He helt it out while I lit it, and then he went and heaved it all to hell. It flowed right through that open front wall where the last one had blowed it out. We waited a minute, and then we heared the blast. It were a bit muffled on account a' it were actual on the inside a' the house. But it done a lot a' damage. The side wall on our left collapsed with the explosion, and most a' the rest a' the roof fell on in. Whenever the dust settled, we looked for any sign a' life, but we never seen any. I looked at Sly.

"Maybe he went out the back door and tuck his horse and ran off," I said.

"We won't know till we go over there," Sly said.

"I ain't anxious to walk in there to what might could be a trap," I said. While we was standing there a-studying on it, Churkee come out. He had heared what we was a-saying.

"You still got one stick a' that dynamite?" he ast me.

"Yeah."

"Let me have it."

I pulled it out and give it to him, wondering what the hell he had in mind. He helt it toward me to light, so I lit it. Then Churkee went to walking over the bridge. He helt that stick out the side as he walked, and he walked right acrost to the other side a' the crick. That fuse was a-sizzling all the way. Then he walked right up the hotel, where the porch had been, and he stepped up and went into the building, or what was left of it. Then he disappeared from view.

In another minute, we seen him come a-running back out like a bat outta hell, and whenever he come to that open space what had used to be a wall, he tuck a headlong dive, and just as he hit the ground a-tumbling, the old hotel blew up, and whenever the blast was a-dying down, so was the old building. There wasn't nothing left over yonder but only a big pile of busted-up boards and stuff. There wasn't no Chugwater to be seen nowhere.

Chapter Nineteen

We all had a real calm and quiet night, even with ole Owl Shit still a-setting in my jailhouse, but I had gone on ahead and turned a-loose all a' my extry depitties. Chugwater were out loose some-wheres, but he didn't have no cowhands left to attack us with. I figgered I'd ride out to his ranch in the morning and see were he hanging around out there or not. I'd take ole Happy with me and leave Butcher to watch the jailhouse and Owl Shit. I'd left Butcher set up overnight to watch Owl Shit anyhow while the rest of us went to our own sweet beds. I, of course, was snuggled down with my sweet nipples Bonnie in our bed upstairs in the Hooch House, and I can tell you, we didn't go right to sleep that night neither.

So in the morning, after I'd had my breakfast and several cups a' hot coffee and a good tall tumbler a' brown whiskey, and Bonnie were still sleeping soundly upstairs, I got holt a' Happy Bonapart, and me and him rid out to Chugwater's place. We rid in real careful, and then we stopped and stared at the house. The place surely did appear to be deserted, but I weren't about to take no unnecessary chances with a skunk like Chugwater.

"Do you think he's there, Barjack?" Happy ast me.

"I don't think, Happy," I said. "I just don't know. All I know for sure is that we never kilt him, and he got outta town."

I nudged my ole horse on and eased him up to the front porch. Happy come along with me. Still a-watching the house, I clumb down outta the saddle. I stood there for a spell once again and stared at the house. Happy follered along. We tied the horses and stepped real easy up onto the porch. There was still nothing, so I put my hand on the door handle and tried it. The door come right open. I let it swing wide, and I drawed out my Merwin Hulbert six-shooter. Happy drawed his Colt. We went on inside, me first and Happy a-follering. We stood there in Chugwater's big living room and looked around. Neither Chugwater nor no one else poked his nose out to see who was messing around in his home. Final I said, "Let's search the place."

We went around from one room to another and we never seen no one. "Barjack," Happy said, "it seems like all a' that fighting and killing was all for nothing. Owl Shit's still a-setting in the jailhouse. Chugwater's lost his entire ranch crew. He's a-loose somewheres, but nothing's really changed except for Chugwater's ranch."

"It weren't all for nothing," I said. "We still got our prisoner. That's what it was all for, and don't never forget that."

"Yes, sir," he said.

We went back outside and climbed onto our horses. Then we rid around the ranch a bit a-looking for any signs a' life. We didn't see none but 'cept cattle. Before we left, I went back inside a' the house and lit it afire. Then we rid off a space and set and watched the place go up in smoke and flames. Chugwater wouldn't have no home to go back to. Well, I didn't want them poor cattle to be neglected and starve, so I had Happy help me, and we driv them on over to my ranch and turned them a-loose with what few animals I had over there. Now I had such a damn big herd I figgered I would have to hire me a crew a' cowboys to watch over them.

I hadn't never wanted to be no big shot cattle man, but now I didn't have much choice. I would have to find me a damn good foreman some-wheres. I set for quite a spell a-studying and con-templating my new herd and thinking about my new status as a rancher. I final reckoned that it was fitting and proper that I was moving up a little in the world. I was already rich, and it weren't quite proper to say that I was a rich marshal and a sa-loon owner. A rancher was a heap more respect-able. So I would become a rancher, and them other two things would just be my sidelines so to speak. At last I tole Happy let's get our ass back to town, and we rid out.

Back in town I had Happy to relieve Butcher, and me and Butcher went on over to the Hooch House and set at my private and personal table. Bonnie were down by that time, and she were a-setting with us. I made up my mind that I were going to get good and drunk that night. Ole Aubrey brung me a tall tumbler a' my favorite whiskey, and I went to work on it. By and by Churkee and his Polly come in and set with us. I ast Churkee what it was he intended to do with his life, and he said that he didn't have no plans.

"What do you know about herding cows?" I said.

"I worked a few ranches back in the Cherokee Nation," he said.

"Could you maybe ramrod a place?"

"If I had one I could," he said, "but I ain't got no money to get a ranch."

"Well," I said, "it just so happens that I got a pretty good one outside a' town. It has a nice little ranch house what just needs a little fixing up, and it's got a good-sized herd a' cattle now. All it needs is a good crew to work it for me. You interested?"

"I reckon I could be," he said.

"I growed up on a ranch," said Polly.

So I figgered it was settled, and I went back to my drinking. By God, I thunk, I had come a long ways for a little snot-nosed kid from New York City what had run away from home on a damn freight train. Well, I went on and got good and drunk that night and slept real good again. Whenever I woked up in the morning, I learnt that Churkee and Polly had went out to my ranch, so I reckoned that it was indeed settled. They had went out and tuck up residence. I were real glad for that, on account a' I could have my big ranch and big herd a' cattle and not have to worry over none a' it. That's the way I wanted it. But I learnt right quick that things was far from settled.

About the middle a' the afternoon, them two come a-riding back into town and found me at my reg'lar spot in the Hooch House. I could tell by the look on their face that they was some kinda trouble. They come up to my table and set their asses down, and, "Barjack," said Churkee, "we got problems out at your ranch."

"What kinda problems we got?" I ast him.

"Me and Polly rode all over the place this morning," he said, "and we never seen one cow."

"Nor a bull nor steer neither," Polly added.

"What?" I said. "There had ought to be a good bunch out there. I had a few, and then me and Happy went and driv all a' Chugwater's cattle over to my place."

"They ain't there now," Churkee said.

"Let me gether up Butcher and Happy and let's all of us ride out there."

So I done that, and the five of us rid out to my ranch. Not that I didn't believe Churkee, but we rid all over the place again just in case, and sure 'nuff, there weren't no cattle nowhere. We couldn't find no sign telling us what had tuck place out there neither. We was just a-setting on our horses and staring out at the empty prairie where all a' my cattle should ought to've been at.

"Churkee," I said.

"What, Barjack?"

"You know, we never did get ole Chugwater."

"And he won't quit, will he?"

"No, sirree," I said, "I don't reckon he will. I should ought to have left one a' these two"—I motioned at Happy and Butcher—"back at the jail to watch over Owl Shit. Chugwater might be hitting there next."

"Should we all get back in there and watch for him?" Butcher said.

"First things first," I said. "Let's think on this problem a' the rustled cattle."

I thunk and thunk as hard as ever I could, and then I recollected that ole Chugwater had a little valley on his place that were kinda hard to get to, and it snugged right up against my own property. A man could run a fair-sized herd into there and block them off pretty easy with some brush and stuff. And all he'd have to do to get them off a' my property would be to just cut a fence.

"Come on," I said. "I got a idee."

I whipped up my ole horse and lit out for that part a' my ranch what was right there where I was a-thinking about. In a while we was there, and sure enough, I seen where my fence had been cut.

"Someone has cut your fence, Barjack," said Happy.

"Tell me something else what ain't readily available to my eyeballs," I said. I kept on a-riding and led the rest right through that cut fence. We rid on down into the valley and by and by we come on the cattle. It looked to me like the whole damn herd.

"Chugwater has reclaimed them," said Churkee, "and he's added yours in too."

"Well, we're a-fixing re-reclaim the bastards,"

I said. "Let's get them moving. Right on through the fence where they've already been through. Come on."

I whipped up my ole horse and the others did the same. We bunched them up first, and then we got them turned in the right direction and started them moving. They bawled and bitched and moaned, but they moved in the right direction. Now and then one ole ornery cow would wander off in her own direction, and one of us would have to chase her back into the herd. We had a few unruly calves to chase down now and then too. It tuck us most a' the afternoon, but we got them back onto my own place, and then we clumb down outta our saddles and mended the damn fence.

I got to wondering who in the hell invented fences in the first place, and it come to me that I would enjoy the hell outta shooting the son of a bitch if I could locate his ass. But we got it did. We rid back to the ranch house, and Churkee and Polly got off a' their horses. "I think we'll just stay right here, Barjack," said Churkee. "I want to keep my eye on that herd. Chugwater might come back, and I ain't hankering to mend that fence again."

"Butcher," I said, "why don't you stay here with them in case there's any more trouble?"

"Yes, sir," he said.

So me and Happy headed back in, now that the cow problem was settled, at least for a time. I had decided to leave Butcher out there with Churkee and Polly on account a' he didn't know nothing about cows and ranches and such, and I figgered he might could learn a little bit by staying out there. And if I was to have just one depitty with me, I had ruther it be Happy than Butcher. I didn't have to worry so much about Happy.

We was riding back into Asininity when Happy ast me, "Do you think it was really Chugwater what cut that fence?"

"Who else?" I said. "He musta seen what we done to his ranch, and he's wanting to get some even. Hell, he might even try to burn my house down out there. Damn. I shoulda warned Churkee about that there possibility."

"If you're right, Barjack," Happy said, "that means that Chugwater's still hanging around these here parts."

"It sure does mean that, Happy," I said, "and with Owl Shit back snug in jail, it means he could be anywhere trying to pull anything. His ranch, my ranch, the jailhouse. Hell, even the Hooch House. Don't forget, Happy, he ain't above turning on women."

"Yes, sir."

We made it back to town, and the first thing we done was we went by the jail and checked on Owl Shit. He were still in his jail cell a-sulking. I figgered he had good reason to sulk, though, on account a' ever' day, he were getting closer to a hanging. "Howdy, Owl Shit," I said. "You ain't saw your brother today, has you?"

"No. I ain't. You blowed him up anyhow."

"No, Owl Shit, we never. We never found no remains we couldn't count for over at that ole hotel."

"Chugwater ain't dead?" he said.

"He's still out there somewheres," I tole him.

"He'll still be a-coming for me," he said.

"I'll be surprised if he don't."

I got the bottle outta my desk drawer and poured me and Happy each a drink, and we set down to drink them. Outta the corner a' my eyeball, I seen Owl Shit with his mouth a-watering, but I wasn't in no mood to take no pity on that son of a bitch. I finished my drink and got up, and I said, "Happy, I want you to stay here in the jailhouse. I'm going out to look around some more."

"Yes, sir," he said.

I went on out, and when I did, I heared Happy say, grumblinglike, to Owl Shit, "Damn your hide, it's your fault I have to stay around here like as if I was in jail." And then I heared Owl Shit laugh. I kept on a-walking, and I never heared no more after that, but I reckon ole Happy done something mean to Owl Shit. It just ain't like Happy to take no guff off a' no damned outlaw.

I hadn't tole Happy, but I never went on back over to the Hooch House. I walked right past it, and I went over to Miss Lillian's fancy eating place. She didn't look none too thrilled to see me a-coming in, and when I ast her for ole Sly, she said he weren't there.

"Well, where might I could find him?" I ast her.

"It wouldn't be too stupid to look at the house," she said. "But don't go inside. Just ask for him at the door. He can go outside to talk to you."

"Yes'm," I said. Now, ain't that a hell of a way to talk to your own ex-wife? Miss Lillian had a way about her to make you act thattaway, though. She

really did. As I walked outta her place a' business,
I reached up and felt a' my ear there where she
had shot a chunk out of it that one time. I walked
on over to the house what had one time been my
house, and there I seen ole Sly a-setting on the
front porch with a cup a' coffee.

"Barjack," he said whenever he spotted me
a-coming, "what brings you around?"

I walked on up to his porch and tuck the other
chair what was setting there. I were panting kinda
hard by this time. I tuck my hat off and mopped
my forehead with a rag I carried in my pocket.

"Sly," I said, "you know, we never got ole Chugwater."

"Yes," he said. "I know."

"He's still around."

I told him about my fence and my cattle. I told
him about leaving Churkee and Polly with
Butcher out to my ranch. I told him that Happy
were minding the jail. "I suppose you're wanting
to go out looking for Chugwater," he said.

"He might try anything," I said. "He might keep
after my cattle, or he might go after Owl Shit. Hell,
he might even go after Bonnie again. You just
never know about that slick son of a bitch."

"You're right, of course," he said. "You want
to ride right now?"

"Yes, I do."

"Just let me go strap on my guns," he said.

Me and Sly rid out to Chugwater's ranch, and
we rid all over that son of a bitch never seeing no
sign a' the bastard we was after. Then we rid to
my place, and I showed him where Chugwater

had cut my fence and where he had driv my herd. I told him how we had brung it back to where it belonged.

"Barjack," Sly said, "the problem is we don't have any idea where he might be hiding, or where he might strike next. I'd maybe say we ought to go back to town and watch out for the jail. That's where his brother is, and his brother's time is running out."

"That's right," I said. "The ole judge could be here any day now, and I reckon that ole Chugwater knows that as well as we do."

"You have Mose Miller and Polly out here at the ranch along with Butcher. They should be able to handle Chugwater if he shows up. Why don't you and I go back to town and watch the jail?"

"Okay, Sly. I can't argue with none a' that. Let's go."

Chapter Twenty

Well, hadn't nothing happened in town, and Happy was a-setting in my chair behint my desk with his damn feet propped up on the desktop a-leaning back and asleep. Owl Shit was a-laying on the cot in the cell. He looked to be asleep too. I walked over to my chair where Happy was a-snoozing, and I put one a' my feet behint one a' the back legs a' the chair. The two front legs was up in the air, and I kinda shoved that back leg forward. Well, the chair turned over backwards with Happy in it, and he hit the foor with a crash. Soon as he come awake, I yelled at him. "Wake up, Happy. The world is coming to a end."

He come a-scrambling to his feet with his eyes kinda glazed, and he said, "What? Where? Where we going?"

"We ain't going nowhere," I said, "but I reckon you're going home to get some shut-eye."

"I'm all right, Barjack," he said. "I ain't seen hide nor hair of ole Chugwater."

"I don't reckon you have," I said. "I don't reckon you've seed much of anything setting there asleep like that."

"Oh, I ain't been asleep. I just dropped off for a minute there. I'm all right."

"I reckon you need to get some sleep," I said, "so go on and do like I tole you to do. I'll stick around here for a spell."

"Well, all right, if you say so."

He went and got his hat off a' the rack and went out the front door. Looking back just before he shut the door behint him, he said, "I'll be back in a little while, Barjack."

Then he went on. I looked at Sly. "There ain't no need for you to hang around here," I tole him. "I can watch the place awhile, I reckon."

"Well," he said, "I guess I'll go see how Lillian is doing. I'll check back with you, though."

He left, so it was just me and ole Owl Shit in the cell. I tuck out my bottle and a tumbler and poured me a full drink. I was just a-setting there and enjoying that good whiskey when I seen Owl Shit kinda stir and then set up. I poured another glass full and tuck it over to him. I guess on account a' I didn't have no other company in there just at that time. He tuck that glass real greedy-like and shaking, and he said, "Thanks, Barjack."

"There ain't nothing like a good glass a' whis-key," I said.

"No, sir," he said. "There ain't."

Well, I dragged a chair over there beside a' the bars, and I set down in it right close to Owl Shit. "Barjack," Owl Shit said, "do you think they're really going to hang me?"

"My guess is that they will, for sure," I tole him. "You know, I seen you shoot that man in cold blood right there in my own saloon, my Hooch House. You never give him a chance or nothing. And I'm bound to give my testimony and to tell it just the way I seen it. There ain't nothing more for it."

"I reckon not," he said, "you being the town marshal and all."

"That's the way of it. Say, Owl Shit, how come you to do people thattaway, to just shoot a man down for nothing like that? What is it that's in you that makes you that mean?"

"I don't know," he said. "I ain't really mean, I don't think."

He drained the rest a' the whiskey outta his glass and stood there looking kinda like a whipped dog. I drained my glass and went after my bottle. When I come back I poured us each one another drink. He tuck a sip.

"People always used to whip up on me when I was a kid," he said, "up until the time I went to carrying my own six-gun, and then one day a big ole boy started in to whip me again, and I shot him. It felt good. It was easy. Each time after that it got easier, you know? Then the next thing I knowed, I didn't even need no excuse. I just shot them if I felt a need to. It made me feel good. That's all."

"How come you to get that name, Owl Shit?" I ast him.

He kinda let his head drop like as if he was a little embarrassed or even ashamed.

"I come home one day whenever I was just a little snot," he said, "and I had stepped in some fresh owl shit out by the barn. I didn't get my shoe cleaned off very good, and my papa smelt it. 'Phew,' he said. 'What's that?' He looked down at my shoe. 'Oh,' I said, 'I just stepped in some fresh owl shit, is all.' Well, from that day, he went to calling me Owl Shit, and ever'one else just kinda picked up on it. I never thought nothing of it, I guess. I was just a little feller."

"I'll be damned," I said. "So it were your own daddy what named you that."

"Yes, sir," he said.

We set there drinking and talking like that till we was both of us pretty damn drunk. After a while, Owl Shit said, "Barjack?"

"What is it?" I said.

"I stepped on that owl shit a purpose. I ain't never tole no one this, but I seen it on the ground, and I just wondered was it soft and would it squish, you know? Like I said, I was just a little snot. So I stepped on it. Sort of to see would it squash?" He paused a bit. Then he said, "It did."

I laughed at that, and he went to laughing too. I poured us another drink. I looked at my bottle, and it were getting kinda low. "Owl Shit," I said, "it looks as how I'm a-going to have to get us another bottle here pretty damn soon." He just nodded his head real slow. "I wish to hell you hadn'ta shot that ole boy right in front a' my eyeballs thattaway," I said. "You know, once you shoot someone thattaway, there ain't no way to un-shoot them. You've done done it, and you're into it then. That's all there is to it, and there ain't nothing can be done about it no more."

"I guess you're right about that."

I drained my glass again, and I went to pour me another drink, but I seen that I woulda tuck the rest a' the booze outta that bottle. I looked over at Owl Shit's glass, and it was empty too. I thunk a minute, and it come into my head that Owl Shit weren't going to live too much longer. I poured the whiskey into his glass and dropped the empty bottle on the floor. I don't know what come into me to make me so generous like that. I felt a little bit foolish for it too. "I got to get us another bottle," I said, but when I went to stand up, I couldn't do it. I just couldn't make my damned ole legs raise me up outta that chair. I got my ass about halfway up and I strained like hell, but then I fell back down kerplop onto the chair.

"Damn," I said.

I studied on the situation for a spell, and then I tuck a holt a' two a' the cell bars what was right there beside a' me, and I tried again, a-pulling myself with the bars, and I managed to get up onto my feet. I stood there for a minute or so just a-getting used to the altitude. My head were spinning. Final I felt kinda steadied up, and I turned toward the door, but the turning had upset something, so I had to stand still again for a bit. Final I decided that I could walk, and I tuck a step with my left foot, but I never went forward. Instead, I kinda lurched sideways and bounced off a' the bars. I steadied myself again and stepped off again, but this time I went way out toward the middle a' the room. Now I didn't have nothing to fall against if I was to fall.

I just stood there with my legs splayed way out,

a-knowing that if I was to try to step off again, I would land flat on my face on that hard floor. I knowed that I had to figger something out pretty damn soon. I thunk that if I was to take another lurching step, this time toward the wall, I could maybe catch myself against the wall and then walk along it back to the bars and back to my chair what was setting over there. Just then the door kinda blowed open and Bonnie come a-swishing into the room. I could smell her perfume soon as she stepped in.

"Barjack," she said.

"Bonnie," I said, "sweet tits, get me to a chair fast."

She rushed over to me and grabbed me and walked me over behint my desk and dropped me in my comfortable chair back there. "What's wrong?" she said.

"Oh," I said, "nothing much. Me and ole Owl Shit was just a-drinking, and we run outta whiskey. Did you bring a bottle with you?"

"No," she said. "I never."

"Well—"

"I can go get you one," she said. "Are you all right? I'll be right back."

"Bring two while you're at it," I said.

She said, "Okay," as she was a-hurrying out the door. I set in my big chair behint my desk, and my head was still a-spinning. I sure did want another drink, and I was pretty sure that Owl Shit did too. I looked over at him, and he had just finished off his. I looked around for my tumbler, and final I seen it a-tumbling around on the floor over by the cell.

"Barjack," Owl Shit said, "are you for sure all right?"

"I'll be just fine, pard," I tole him, "whenever ole Bonnie gets back here with my whiskey."

It weren't long before she come back with two bottles, and while she were a-picking up my tumbler for me I opened up one bottle. I poured me a drink and tuck a big slug of it, and by God, I was right. I were some better as soon as I done that. I got my ass up and went back over to my chair by the jail cell, and I poured ole Owl Shit another drink.

"Barjack," said Bonnie, kinda snappy like, "what are you doing?"

"I'm just setting over here getting drunk with ole Owl Shit," I said.

"Ain't you got no work you'd ought to be a-doing?"

"I'm a-doing it," I said. "I'm watching the jail. I sent Happy home to get him some sleep."

"Well, I sure have been missing you over at the Hooch House."

"Set your ass down here and have a drink with us," I said.

She went over to my desk drawer and got herself a tumbler. Then she dragged a chair over beside me, and I poured her a drink. She kinda sipped at it and that were all right. I knowed if she drank too much a' my whiskey too fast, she'd be drunk on her fat ass right quicklike. She were used to them sissy pink things what Aubrey mixed up for her. But she weren't above sipping my whiskey if that was all what we had. At first Bonnie was a little bit kinda setting back from the conversation and all. It were clear to me that she did not approve a' my drinking like that with ole Owl Shit. After all, he was a killer, a murderer. I had arrested him and throwed his ass in jail. And we'd had all a' that killing on account a' him. It was his own brother what was giving us all a' this trouble. So Bonnie somehow did not approve a' me a-drinking with him.

She had her own self set her ass down to drink with us, but she had me betwixt her and Owl Shit, and she weren't talking neither. She were just kinda sipping her whiskey with a real hard and stubborn look on her fat face. Ever now and then I would say something to Owl Shit and then I'd look over at Bonnie and say, "Now, ain't that right, sweetness?" She wouldn't say nothing. I got a little fed up with all a' that cold shoulder, and I reached over and put my left arm around her and hugged her over to me and kissed her on the side a' her chubby face.

"Don't, Barjack," she said, and she shoved me away real hard until I was knocked plumb against the cell bars. Well, hell, at least I had got her to talk. By and by Happy come back in, and he did look like he was awake by then.

"Happy," I said, "are you ready to take back over?"

"Yes, sir, I am."

"Good, 'cause I'm just about ready to pass on out."

Owl Shit stood up and tuck a staggering couple a' steps toward the cot. "Me too," he said, and he fell down on the cell floor. He looked comfy enough, so I decided to just let him lay there. I don't much know what happened after that. I recall trying to stand up again, and Bonnie a-helping me, but the next thing I know, I was a-waking up, and I was on the cot a' that other cell. Bonnie was a-setting in a chair she had put just beside the cot. I reckon she had set there all night. She were a loving thing, she were. I could tell pretty soon by the noises and such that Happy or someone was a-making some coffee in the main room. I was sure enough glad a' that. I set up with a moan and Bonnie come awake.

"Barjack," she said.

"I'm just fine," I said. "Soon as that coffee's did out there, I'll be great."

"It won't be long, Barjack," said Happy, calling out from the other room.

"Goddamn," I said, "are you spying on me out there?"

Happy poked his face into the cell. "No, sir, I could just hear you whenever you talked, is all. I wasn't spying."

I stood up and were just a little bit wobbly. I wouldn't say that I had a hangover. I never had no hurting head nor nothing like that. I think that maybe I were still just a little bit drunk from the night before. Anyhow, I stood there a minute a-getting my bearings, and then I walked on out into the main room. Happy was a-sweeping the floor. I didn't like the dust in the air none, so I said, "Happy, that's enough a' that." He put the broom in a corner a' the room. I went on behint my desk to set down, and I seen that Owl Shit was still a-laying in the floor. He didn't look to me like he had stirred one little bit all night long.

I looked at the clock on my wall, and I couldn't read it for it being so blurry. "What time is it?" I ast.

Happy said, "It's ten thirty." Then it come to me. I hadn't been paying no attention to it on account a' all the trouble we'd been having, but today was of a sudden the day the judge was supposed to be a-hitting town.

"Happy," I said, "wake Owl Shit up. The judge is coming in today. We got to have Owl Shit ready for court. And don't throw no water on him. He ain't got a change a' clothes here."

"Yes, sir," Happy said, and he unlocked the cell door and went inside to wake up Owl Shit, and it tuck him some time to do it too. "What's the matter here?" he said. "You ain't woke me up like this here before."

"Owl Shit," I said, "I'm sorry to have to tell you this, but today is your court day. The judge is a-coming into town today."

He set up a-looking real sober. His back was straight and his face was serious. "Couldn't someone ride out to the ranch house and get me a clean shirt?" he said.

"Owl Shit," I said, "we burnt your house to the

ground. You ain't got a clean shirt." I thunk for a minute, and then I said, "Happy, run over to the gen'ral store and have ole Suder come over here."

Happy run and got Suder, and when Suder come into the office I had him take a good look at Owl Shit, and I said, "He's got to go to court today, Suder. Can you go back over to your store and pick him out some good clothes?"

"Yes, sir," he said, and he went to studying on ole Owl Shit. Then I sent for a barber, and whenever we got all through, Owl Shit looked like as if he were a-going to teach a Sunday school class. He was damn near pretty. He were almost a-feared to set down for fear a' wrinkling his new britches. Course, I charged ever'thing to Peester's office, knowing that I'd hear about it later from him, the pettifogging bastard.

"Barjack?" said Happy. He were standing at the front winder.

"What?" I said.

"Who's that a-coming into town?"

I went over to have a look. It were a skinny old man a-riding on a mule. He was a-wearing a black suit and a stovepipe hat, and he had a full beard all over his face. "That there's the judge," I said. He were riding straight toward my office too.

Chapter Twenty-one

Well, we filled that scraggy ole judge in on ever'thing what had done happened regarding Owl Shit and Chugwater, and he kinda shuck his head and grumbled. He said, "That ain't the way we likes to have things done around here, but I reckon it just couldn'ta been helped. This, uh, Chugwater, is he still a-running loose?"

"Yes, he is, Your Honor," I said, "we been a-chasing him, but he just seems to 'a' disappeared. Can't find him nowheres."

"You'll have to keep after him until you catch or kill him," the judge said. "It's too bad we can't have him and his brother on trial at the same time."

"Yes, sir," I said.

"How many deputies do you have, Barjack?"

"I have two reg'lar depitties," I said. "In rare cases like this one here we been a-talking about, I can raise up a few more special depitties. I had five extries on this Chugwater case, but I've done let them go on account a' we ain't even seed Chugwater now for some time."

"What about the county sheriff?"

"I went to him for help, but he just downright refused me," I told him.

"Hmm. I'll have a talk with him about that. Well, we'll have the trial right away, say, ten o'clock in the morning."

And we did too, and it were brief. I was the main witness against ole Owl Shit being as how he had shot that man down right smack in front a' me, and I told the tale just how it happened too. I was a little bit sad to have to do that, on account a' I had growed some fond a' that worthless shit, Owl Shit, and I was a-going to be the main reason a' his neck stretching, but I done my duty, and I tole the tale. There was a few more witnesses what had saw the thing happen, and they tole it their way too. Owl Shit didn't have no lawyer, but it wouldn'ta done him no good if he had. Whenever the judge asked him if he had anything to say for hisself, he stood up in his shackles and coughed. Then he looked right at the judge, and he said, "I didn't think I was doing no one no harm when I shot that man. Hell, he was a stranger around here. No one knowed him, so the way I see it is that there wasn't no one around here what had the right to file no complaint on me. This here case had ought to be dismissed. That's how I see it."

Course the judge didn't see it thattaway. He sentenced Owl Shit to be hanged out to dry. Owl Shit jumped up and yelled, "I won't never hang. My brother will be back, and he'll kill ever' one a' you bastards."

The judge found Owl Shit guilty a' contempt a'

court, but it didn't seem to me that there was no use in that. Owl Shit didn't have no money, and he was going to hang up anyhow, so what the hell? I damn near put my hand in my pocket to find enough cash to pay the fine, but I never. We tuck Owl Shit back to the jail cell and locked him up to wait for his hanging time. He sulked the whole time. I went and got drunk that night, and the judge went on toward the county seat. I tried to imagine the scene with the ole judge a-chewing out ole Dick Cody for refusing to give me a hand against ole Chugwater. It made me chuckle to think about it.

We went and had a actual gallows built up in Asininity. We had never did that before. We hadn't had no need for it in quite a spell, and way back when we did have a need, we had just used a overhanging beam somewheres on the roof overhang over the boardwalk or else a tree branch when we could find one. But we hired a goddamn good carpenter, ole Billy by Damn, well, his real name was Billy Burton, but we all just always called him Billy by Damn, and he was a hell of a good carpenter. He put up a damn fine gallows too. I was just about sad that we would have to tear it down. I wisht we had some more to string up along with Owl Shit. It just seemed like to me a crying shame to have such a fine thing constructed by a fine craftsman like Billy by Damn, and then to not keep it around. Billy, he didn't mind, though, on account a' he was going to be paid to build the thing, and he was going to get the joy a' watching his creation in use, and he was a-going to get paid again for tearing it down. On top a' that, he was going to be able to keep all the material too and reuse it however he might want to, all the lumber, the nails, hell, even the rope.

I decided that ole Billy had ought to make even more money, so I ast him if he would like to pull the handle to spring the trapdoor when the day come, and he grinned real big and said, "Yes, by damn, I surely would." So we agreed how much I would pay him for that little job. Actual, it would be Peester who would pay him, not me.

Well, Owl Shit had to set in his cell and listen to Billy by Damn a-pounding nails and sawing boards all day long ever' day a-knowing that what was going up was the scaffold which he would climb up onto to be swung out to the end a' his rotten life. It come to me that it was a gruesome practice which we in law enforcement was a-practicing. I decided that if it was left up to me, what I would do would be to sentence them to death and then take them out in the street and shoot them dead right then and there and be quick about it.

Well, the day and the time final come, and Billy by Damn was outside a-sanding on the gibbet. I checked the time, and I sent a rider out for Churkee, Polly, and Butcher. When they final arrived in from the ranch, I said, "That's it. This job has got to be did. It's time for the hanging." He stopped his sanding and run inside, where he washed his face and hands in the bowl in the back room. Then he put on a tie and a coat and a derby hat. He looked kinda silly, I thunk, but he were just a-trying to be in the right spirit for the occasion.

Well, I pulled on my black coat and hat, and even ole Happy and ole Butcher, they done the same. We was a somber-looking bunch, I can tell you. We went into the cell and handcuffed Owl Shit's hands behint his back, and then I went to doing a solemn march out to the gibbet. Butcher and Happy, one on each side a' him, marched Owl Shit along behint me. Billy by Damn come along last. We didn't have no preacher on account a' Owl Shit had done run him off, calling him all kinda foul names as he was a-running away.

I walked up the stairs, and my depitties with the condemned man come right behint me. Billy dropped off below and went to the death handle. He stood there a-looking real by damn proud a' hisself. Happy and Butcher placed Owl Shit right on the trapdoor, and I stepped up behint him. I read the death warrant out loud so ever'one in the crowd what had gathered up in the street to gawk could hear it, and then I ast Owl Shit if he wanted to say any last words. "Just hang my ass," he said.

"Do you want a hood?" I ast him.

"Hell, no," he said. "I want to look ever'one in the eye what's a-looking at me."

"Have it your way," I said, and I fitted the noose down over his head and around his neck, snugging the knot down tight just behint his left ear. Then I walked to the front a' the platform in order for Billy by Damn to be able to see me whenever I motioned to him to pull the handle. But I reckon that he had forgot his instructions, on account a' as soon as he seed me step to the front, he pulled the damn thing. The trapdoor dropped. The noise startled me, and I looked around real quicklike just in time to see Owl Shit's head disappear down the hole and the rope go tight, and I think I even heared a loud cracking sound what was likely Owl Shit's neck a-snapping. A big gasp went through the crowd. Some women hid their faces like they would ruther not have saw the scene, but then, why was they there?

I motioned Happy and Butcher to go on down, and then I started down. It were prob'ly a strange time for it, but I was a-thinking about what a hell of a fine job Billy had did on the building a' that platform. It were solid. Not a board squeaked whenever I walked on it and down the stairs. I looked underneath whenever I got down to the street again, and I seed Owl Shit's carcass a-swinging gently in the breeze. He looked dead, for damn sure. I ain't said nothing about it yet, but all the time I was looking over the crowd and even the whole street a-watching out for Chugwater. I never seed nothing of him.

I walked straight down to the Hooch House. Along the way, Bonnie caught up with me and tuck me by my right arm. She had been in the crowd a-watching. "You done good, sweetie," she said.

"It ain't a job I'm proud of," I said.

We went on inside and set down at my private table in my own private chairs, and Aubrey seen us coming and brung our drinks right fast. I can't recall a time when I felt so much like I was in need of a glass a' good whiskey. I gulped it right down, and he brung me another one. Dingle come in a-scribbling as he walked. He bumped right smack into a great big workingman a' some kind. Lucky for Dingle the man din't have no bad temper. He just tuck Dingle by the upper arms and lifted him up into the air, moved him over and set him down again. Then he went on his way, and Dingle, still a-scribbling, come on back to my table and set his ass down. Sly came in, and right after him, both my depitties. Churkee and Polly final come around and the gang was complete. It was quiet, though. Sly final said something.

"Barjack," he said, "do you think that, now that Owl Shit is dead, Chugwater will stop?"

"It seems like he done has," I said.

"I know that his main reason was to try to save his brother," Sly said, "but my question is now that reason is gone, will he quit, or will he go on to seek revenge?"

"I don't know the man that good, Widdamaker," I said. "I wisht I did."

"I think I seen ever'body except Chugwater at the hanging," Happy said.

"I wonder if I'd get a big crowd like that at my hanging," said Butcher.

"You planning to hang, Butcher?" Happy said.

"No, I ain't, but I mean, if ever'one knew I was going to die, would so many show up to watch me do it?"

Aubrey come over to serve ever'one drinks, and he brung me a third. I looked over at Churkee. "How's things out at the ranch?" I ast him.

"We haven't had any more trouble, Barjack. The fence is still down, but we've mixed all the cattle together and we're using Chugwater's pasture for them. I think we'll need to hire a couple a' men at least."

"Go on ahead and hire them," I said.

"Okay."

Peester come in, and he come straight back to my table. "Barjack," he said, "congratulations on a job well done. I'm sure that everyone in Asininity is glad to have it over with and done so successfully."

Just at that there time, I couldn't think a' nothing mean to say to the old pettifogger. I just looked up at him and said, "Thank you, Mr. Mayor. Would you care to set down with us and have a drink?"

"Well, I don't—"

"On the house?"

"Thank you," he said, and he pulled out a chair and set down. I waved at Aubrey, and he come over. The mayor seed the pink sissy drink Bonnie was having, and he ast for one a' them. I still never teased him nor picked on him. There would always be another time.

Just then there was a loud bang. It sounded to me like a shotgun blast. It was loud enough, and it was so unexpected, that it made me jump. "That sounded like a shotgun," said Sly.

I looked down at Happy. "Happy," I said, "you and Butcher go check it out."

They both jumped up and said, "Yes, sir." They went a-running out. We all went quiet again after that. I noticed that Peester had jumped at the sound too, and he had spilt his pink sissy drink down the front a' his white suit. In another minute, Happy come back in. He was a-carrying what looked like a letter in his hand. He come back to the table, and he give me the letter.

"It looked like Chugwater, Barjack," he said.

"What do you mean, looked like?"

"Well, it's the right size and all, and it's wearing what looks to me like Chugwater's clothes."

"What is? Goddamn it, Happy, don't you know how to tell a story?"

"Well," he said, "just around the corner we found a corpus. It appears that it has shot its own self right smack in the head. Like he stuck the shotgun barrels right up under his chin and blowed his whole face off. But like I said, its clothes and all, it looks to me like it's Chugwater."

He handed the paper to me. It were really one paper and one envelope already sealed. The paper was a note. It said "Will some kind soul please mail this letter for me?" It weren't signed. I tossed it on the table and looked at the envelope. It were addressed to a woman in Indiana. I couldn't reckanize the name. I tore it open and tuck the letter out.

Dear Aint Sally,

As you are my mama's only living relative, I am writing to you, this my final communication to the world. I made my mama a solemn promise as she was a-laying on her deathbed. I promised that I would always take good keer of little Mer-

win. I tried, and I done real good up till now. Just today, they hung him for a killing he done. I tried to prevent it, but I failed. So I'm leaving this world with him, and I hope to see him and Mama in the next world. Forgive me for your sister, please. Good by.

Your nephew,

Chug (This was scratched out.)

Charlton

I read it out loud to ever'one at the table. "So he did make the hanging," said Sly.

"The poor son of a bitch," I said. "Couldn't keep his promise to his mama, so he blowed his face off."

Withdrawn

For Every
Individual...

Renew by Phone
269-5222

Renew on the Web
www.imcpl.org

For General Library Infomation
please call 275-4100

CPSIA information can be obtained at www.ICGtesting.com
Printed in the USA
269884BV00003B/3/P